BREAKING RULES

DELTA FORCE STRONG BOOK #2

ELLE JAMES

TWISTED PAGE INC

BREAKING RULES

DELTA FORCE STRONG BOOK #2

New York Times & *USA Today*
Bestselling Author

ELLE JAMES

EBOOK ISBN: 978-1-62695-330-7

PRINT ISBN: 978-1-62695-300-0

Dedicated to my incredibly swift and efficient editor (also my sister) Delilah Devlin.
And to my personal assistant who manages my life and keeps me moving forward, Nora.
And to my dogs for allowing me brief spurts of their nap time so that I can write my words!

AUTHOR'S NOTE

Enjoy other military books by Elle James

Delta Force Strong
Ivy's Delta (Delta Force 3 Crossover)
Breaking Silence (#1)
Breaking Rules (#2)
Breaking Away (#3)
Breaking Free (#4)
Breaking Hearts (#5) coming soon

Visit ellejames.com for more titles and release dates
For hot cowboys, visit her alter ego Myla Jackson at
mylajackson.com
and join Elle James's Newsletter at
https://ellejames.com/contact/

CHAPTER 1

"I DON'T SEE any sign of the dealer or anyone else, for that matter," Delta Force Sergeant Ryan "Dash" Hayes spoke softly into his mic. As point man for the mission, he was the farthest forward and in the most precarious position. If their target showed up with a full contingent of Taliban gunmen, he could be in trouble.

"According to our Intel guys, he's supposed to be there right about now," said Sergeant Rucker Sloan, the team lead. "Dash, you sure he's not there already and we missed him?"

"I'm sure. It's dead out there. Nothing moving."

"You think someone tipped them off?" Bull's voice came across.

"Could be," Dash said. "Unless they show up in the next thirty minutes, I'd say they aren't coming."

"We've already been here for thirty," Lance's voice

sounded in Dash's ear. "I say we leave before we're discovered."

A snort sounded in Dash's ear. "You just want to get back to the forward operating base," Dash drawled.

"Yeah, so?" Lance said.

"It's not like you're going to get to meet Miss Daye in person. She'll have men all around her."

"It would be nice to hear her sing. We rarely get to see the USO tours," Lance said. "It would be nice to see one with Sunny Daye in it. I saw her and her partner, Ray Bonner, in concert in Austin last year. They were phenomenal."

"I thought Ray died." Dash shifted in his position, his gaze on the warehouse building in front of him but his mind on the beautiful singer, Sunny Daye. "I thought Miss Daye quit singing after her partner's death."

"She did," Lance said. "For a few months. Then she joined the USO in an effort to give back."

"I heard she joined to get out of the States and away for the paparazzi," Craig "Bull" Bullington said.

"Probably a little bit of both," Lance said. "She was pretty broken up about losing her partner. They made some really good music together."

"I think she carried the pair," Rucker said over the radio. "He didn't have as powerful a voice."

With his thoughts on the beautiful Sunny Daye, it

was half a second before Dash realized a vehicle was heading his way. "Guys, we got company."

All chatter ceased.

"What do you have?" Rucker asked.

"A cargo truck."

Mac snorted in Dash's ear. "The question is, what kind of cargo?"

"If they're delivering at this location, we can only hope our middleman shows," Rucker said. "From what Nora said, and what the intelligence reports indicate, the man is American."

"He's not American," Dash said through his teeth. "He's an animal."

"Truth," Rucker said. "Any man dealing in human trafficking is nothing more than an animal."

"Pond scum," Dawg said. "I have my sights set on the truck. If our target steps one foot out, I'll blow his fuckin' head off."

"It would be better if you just wound him," Rucker warned. "We need him so the intelligence guys can follow the chain of lowlifes who are perpetuating this travesty. Selling little girls and women into the sex trade is as low as you get."

"Yeah, but after they get all the information out of him, we need to turn him loose in a minefield," Blade said. "He needs to die a painful, bloody death."

"The truck is pulling to the back of the building." The vehicle moved out of Dash's view.

"Dawg, you got eyes on it?"

"I do," Dawg responded. "The driver's backing up to a loading ramp. Driver and front passenger just got out. They're going in a side door. An overhead door is rolling up." Dawg paused in his reporting. "Bastards," he murmured.

"What's happening?" Rucker asked.

"They're herding women and children into the building," Dawg said. "I count four guards with AK-47 rifles."

"Move in," Rucker said. "We want to help the women and children, but, above all, we want to catch the guy orchestrating these trades."

The Delta team moved in, creeping silently toward the building and the men who were moving their captives.

Anger burned inside Dash. How any man could trade humans like animals, he just couldn't understand. They had to be animals themselves.

His rifle at the ready, he eased closer to the building.

"All in?" Rucker murmured in Dash's ear.

One by one, the Delta team acknowledged in low, steady tones.

"Let's do this," Rucker said.

The building wasn't like the others in the area. It had been recently constructed of metal, more like warehouse buildings in the States. It stood on the edge of the village, a big box of a metal building, seeming out of place among the mud-and-stick resi-

4

dential Afghan homes.

Dash and Blade were first in, taking out the two guards left standing on the loading dock, supposedly guarding the open overhead door.

"Dock's clear," Dash reported after dragging the guard off to the side to avoid setting off any alarms.

The team entered the building through the large overhead doors.

Their goal wasn't to kill all the men handling the women and children. They were there to capture the guy making the deals. However, if they killed a few of the bastards, great. Men like that didn't belong in the world.

With strict instructions from their CO, they were to limit collateral damage. That meant they couldn't shoot into the crowd of women and children. They might be shot at, but they couldn't shoot back and risk the lives of any innocents.

The men inside were busy lining up the women and children. They marched a woman up to a raised platform.

One of the men grabbed the scarf from her head and ripped the abaya from her shoulders. The garment fell to the floor.

The woman squealed and tried to reach for the folds of fabric, but the man twisted his hand in her hair and yanked her upright.

Tears streamed from her eyes as she stood naked in front of a small group of men in turbans. She tried unsuccessfully to cover herself with her hands and arms.

The men standing below the poor woman approached her, studied her body and leaned their heads together. Finally, one nodded and spoke in what sounded more like Arabic than Pashtu.

The man holding the woman's hair allowed her to gather her garments. Then he shoved her to the end of the dais and off to the side.

Another man lifted a female child up onto the raised platform.

"Bastards," Dash murmured. "They're selling these women and children."

"Do you see our American middleman?"

Dash scanned the crowd of men, women and children. In the far corner of the building, another man stood, leaning his back against the wall, wearing a brown, felt Fedora, khaki cargo pants and a long-sleeved, loose-fitting shirt. His wardrobe stood out among the men dressed in the baggy trousers and tunics of middle eastern men.

"Back right corner," Dash said.

"I see him," Rucker responded from his position on the other side of the door leading into the warehouse. "Mac, Tank, Blade, Lance…cover the rear exit. Bull, Dash and I are going in."

"Roger," Mac responded. "On our way around the outside."

Before Rucker and Bull could join Dash, the man in the Fedora spun and walked toward the rear exit.

Dash swore. "Our target just headed for the exit."

"Picking up the pace," Mac said. "See him ahead. He's getting into a dark SUV."

"Cripple it, but keep the bastard alive," Rucker whispered.

"He discharged five men from the SUV. They're providing cover for the vehicle's getaway," Mac reported.

"Do whatever it takes," Rucker said. "We have to catch the bastard. We're aborting the show and heading your way. Come on, Bull, Dash. Our guy is getting away."

Dash's jaw hardened. He hated leaving the women and children under such dire circumstances, but they had to catch the American responsible for selling them. Once they had him in hand, they'd go back to help the others.

After backing quietly out of the warehouse, Dash and Rucker turned and ran toward the back of the building.

The sound of machine gun rounds ripped through the air before Rucker and Dash reached the corner. They stopped short and pressed their backs to the wall. It was only a matter of time before the other men inside came out to see what all the fuss was about.

"Dawg, what's going on? Where's our target?" Rucker's demanded.

"I fired on the driver's side window and the tires, but the SUV is still moving. Hard to see in the dark to get a good bead on the tires when they're driving directly away from me. The others are pinned down. The opposition is heavily armed, two bearing machine guns. When any of our guys move, they throw everything at them."

In the lead, Dash eased up to the edge of the building, fit his night vision goggles over his eyes and glanced around the corner.

He spotted the green heat signatures of Mac, Blade, Tank and Bull, lying low to the ground, returning fire when they could.

Looking past them, he spotted four of the five men Dawg had indicated. They appeared as small green blobs hunkered close to the ground, their weapons trained on the Deltas.

Beyond them were the taillights of the SUV leaving the scene before they could capture the one person they wanted most.

Dash shook his head. How had the man managed to leave behind a team of heavily armed men? Had he known the Deltas were there? Was that why he'd left in such a hurry?

"Dawg," Rucker said. "Forget the SUV. Cover our guys until we can put a plug in those machine guns. We'll cover anyone coming out of the building."

"Will do," Dawg said.

Rucker, Bull and Dash turned away from their teammates.

"I'll cover the other end of the building," Dash said.

"If you step out now, they'll nail you," Rucker warned.

"I'm not stepping out. I'll go low and fast," he assured Rucker. "Cover me."

"I've got your six," Rucker said.

Using his elbows and knees, Dash low-crawled to the other end of the building, his rifle cradled in front of him. Once there, he rounded the corner and established a position covering the opposite side.

Between rapid bursts of bullets, a single shot rang out.

Dash glanced behind him.

The first shot hit one of the five men firing on the Deltas. His machine gun went silent.

Checking for trouble in front of him, Dash watched, waiting for the remaining men to leave the women and children and come out to defend their buddies.

The next shot silenced the second machine gun. A quick glance to his rear reassured Dash that the three remaining men had eased backward. He couldn't make out their heat signatures.

But that didn't mean they weren't there.

With fewer rounds being fired, Dash picked up on other sounds.

Engines revved.

Dash ran along the side of the building to the front.

The vehicles that had been parked there earlier were leaving, spinning up dirt and gravel as they took off.

The engine of the truck that had brought the women and children to the warehouse roared to life.

Instead of helping the other gunmen, the men who'd been inside herding their cargo were now loading the women and children into the truck. They shouted orders, pushed and shoved them into the truck about to pull away from the loading dock.

"The truck's getting ready to leave," Dash said into his mic.

"Do what you can to stop it," Rucker said. "We're on our way."

Dash aimed at the man still standing on the dock. This was the man who'd stripped the first woman on the dais. Now, he held a child in his arms. He swung her around and tossed her into the back of the truck like a sack of potatoes, the last child to be loaded.

Dash pulled the trigger, taking the bastard down with a single shot. Another man appeared. Dash took him down.

The truck lumbered away from the dock, slowly picking up speed.

"Rucker, are you in position?" Dash asked.

"We're here," Rucker said.

"Cover me. I'm going to stop that truck."

"Bull will provide cover," Rucker said. "I'll take the passenger side."

"I've got the driver." His jaw tight, Dash raced for the driver's door as Rucker went for the passenger side.

They arrived at the same time, climbing up on the step.

Dash yanked open the driver's door.

The driver yelled in surprise and tried to shove Dash away.

On the other side of the cab, Rucker had jerked open the passenger door. He was wrestling the weapon out of the man's hand when it went off, blasting a hole through the windshield.

Dash clamped his arm around the driver's neck and snapped his head to one side. The driver went limp. The truck lurched forward as the man's foot rested hard on the accelerator. As he slumped to the side, his arms turned the steering wheel.

Dash fought to pull the driver out of his seat. When he couldn't, he crawled on top of him, shoved the guy's foot to the side, took control of the steering wheel and found his way to the brake.

Rucker had the passenger in a death grip, fighting for control of the rifle in his hands.

When Dash jerked the steering wheel around,

Rucker slammed the butt of his rifle into the passenger's face, knocking him out. Grabbing the man's arm, he pulled him out of the cab. He fell to the ground and rolled beneath the truck's wheels.

The truck bounced over the man, nearly jerking the steering wheel out of Dash's hands.

When he had the vehicle under control, he pressed his foot on the brake and brought the truck to a gradual stop.

Before the vehicle came to a complete halt, Rucker was out of the cab and on the ground, headed to the rear.

Dash set the parking brake and joined Rucker at the back of the vehicle.

A man bearing an AK-47 leaped to the ground and ran into the dark.

In the bed of the truck, women and children scrambled to get their feet beneath them, some of them whimpering in pain, others sobbing in fear.

"Mac?" Rucker said into his mic.

"All clear at the warehouse. Dawg got the main gunners. We cleaned up another. Anyone left standing bugged out."

"We stopped the truck," Rucker said. "Like you said, anyone left standing bugged out."

The men gathered around the truck and checked the status of all the people inside. Other than a few bruises and scrapes, they were intact. Shaken, scared and tearful, but alive.

"You gonna make the call?" Dash asked Lance, their radio guy.

Lance nodded. "On it." He placed the radio call to the helicopters. Moments later, two Black Hawk helicopters landed near the warehouse.

Within the next few minutes, Dash, Lance, Blade and Dawg climbed aboard one of the choppers.

Rucker, Bull, Tank and Mac stayed behind to drive the truck back to the forward operating base where a team from the Intelligence unit and representatives of the local Afghan government would meet them and take the women and children to a temporary shelter.

At least that was what they were told. Dash wasn't sure what to believe. As little as the men of the Middle East thought of their women, he couldn't be sure of their treatment.

Dash buckled his safety harness and leaned back. The mission hadn't gone according to plan. The American traitor, who had been coordinating the sale of humans into slavery and the sex trade, was still free to continue his nefarious operation. They'd been so close. Dash knew close was only good if you were throwing hand grenades.

Lance clapped his hands together and grinned, always the optimist. "We should be back in time for the tail end of the USO concert. I'm going to see if I can meet Sunny Daye in person."

"Won't she be surrounded by bodyguards?" Dash asked.

Lance shrugged. "Probably, but I'm good at finding my way around obstacles. A couple of bodyguards won't slow me down."

"I hear they have strict rules," Dawg said. "You can be court-martialed for breaking them."

Dash grinned. Something about rules made him want to break them. Especially if they didn't make a whole lotta sense. "More than likely, we've missed the concert. She's probably already packed up and left the base for her next stop."

"The woman has to sleep sometime," Blade noted.

Dash leaned his head back and let the vibration of the rotors lull him into a state of half-sleep.

It was after midnight when the chopper made it back to the base. Well past curfew for those who weren't working the night shift or standing guard at the gates or on perimeter.

Dash was ready for a shower and his rack.

The stage that had been erected earlier that day was gone from the exercise field. Trucks stood in a line ready to head out in the morning.

"Damn. They break down fast," Lance remarked as the helicopter pilot slowly lowered the aircraft to the ground.

"They don't mess around," Blade said. "Too bad we missed the show. I would've liked seeing Sunny Daye perform. I hear she puts on a good show."

"Yeah, me, too," Dawg said. "You think we can convince the CO to schedule a mission close to her next stop?"

"I wish," Dash said. "Right now, I could use a sandwich and a shower…in that order."

"I'm hitting the shower," Lance said.

"Don't hog all the hot water," Dash warned. "On second thought, maybe I'll get that shower first."

"You'll have to race me to it," Lance said, unbuckling his safety harness before the chopper touched the ground.

As soon as the aircraft landed, Lance and Dash were out the door, racing for their quarters.

Dash could care less about getting to the shower unit first, but he needed the adrenaline rush to clear his head after their failed mission. Whoever it was negotiating the sales of those women and children knew how to cover his own ass. He'd come prepared with his own protection and got away because of it.

It burned in Dash's gut that they hadn't caught the guy. How many more lives would he destroy before he was finally brought to justice. And it fired Dash's ass that the man was apparently American.

If Rucker's girl, Nora Michaels, hadn't been caught in one of his raids and escaped, they wouldn't have known that much. She hadn't seen his face, but she'd heard his voice and accent before she'd escaped with the little girls he'd stolen from an orphanage.

The man was slippery and completely heartless. He had to be stopped.

Racing toward their temporary quarters where they'd stashed their go bags, Blade veered right to his tent, while Dash veered left and rounded the corner of a building. Before he could stop himself, he ran into the back of someone carrying a heavy object over his shoulder. The person and his burden crashed to the ground with a grunt.

Dash landed on what appeared to be a body bag like the ones used to ship dead servicemen back to the states. He struggled to untangle his weapon from the squirming contents.

The man he'd knocked to the ground crawled out from under the bag and Dash, leaped to his feet and tore off, running away as fast as he could.

By the time Dash rose to his feet with his weapon in his hands, the man had disappeared around the corner of a row of tents.

Dash started after him.

"Help," a voice called out behind him.

Someone from inside the squirming body bag the man had been carrying called out, "Please, help."

Halted in his tracks by the decidedly feminine tone, Dash fought the urge to go after the man. Instead, he remained where he was and searched for an opening.

Holding his rifle in one hand, he pulled at a zipper. A female emerged, with curves in all the right places and a mane of shiny, light-colored hair that had turned a shadowy blue in the moonlight.

She wasn't wearing a desert camouflage uniform, nor was she wearing Army PT shorts and a shirt. Instead, she wore sparkling high heels, a short skirt and sequined tank top.

What the hell?

He held out his hand.

When she placed hers in his, he hauled her to her feet.

She swayed and fell against his chest, tears smearing the makeup on her face. "Oh my God. Thank you," she cried, wrapping her arms around him.

Footsteps pounded, racing toward them.

Dash slipped his arm around the woman and turned his body to shield her with his, bringing his rifle up to point at the owners of the footsteps rounding the corner of the building.

Two uniformed soldiers with black military police armbands, four men in black leather jackets and Dash's Delta teammate, Blade, skidded to a stop at the end of his rifle barrel.

"Dash, someone abducted Sunny Daye," Blade's wide eyes narrowed. "Hey, why are you pointing your rifle at us?"

Dash lowered his weapon and moved slightly, exposing the woman he'd found in the body bag.

His arm still around her, he frowned down into her eyes. "I take it you're Miss Daye."

She nodded, her arms slipping around his waist. For a moment, she held him close. Then she squared her shoulders and lifted her chin, swiping at her wet, makeup-smeared cheeks. "That's right. I'm Sunny, and this man saved my life."

CHAPTER 2

SUNNY DAYE STOOD close to the man in the combat uniform, helmet and bulletproof vest, feeling safer than she'd felt since she'd stepped foot on the arid soil of Afghanistan. "You know who I am… I'd like to know the name of the man who saved me from being carried away in that…that…bag." She shivered as she stared down at the dark bag someone had thrown over her head.

"Jesus, Dash." A man, dressed like the one who'd saved her shook his head. "That's a body bag."

Sunny's blood chilled, and she shook uncontrollably.

Her rescuer pulled her up against him, his arm securely around her waist.

All four of her bodyguards frowned and took a step closer.

She held up her hand. "I'm okay. But I wouldn't

have been if this man hadn't tackled the man who'd grabbed me." She looked up at him. "Is your name really Dash?"

The soldier's lips twitched. "That's what my friends call me." He held out his free hand. "Sergeant Ryan Hayes, at your service. You can call me Dash, if you like."

She removed her arm from around his waist and took his hand in hers. "Dash, words aren't enough thanks for what you did. But, thank you." She leaned up on her toes to kiss his cheek.

Before her lips touched his camouflage painted face, he turned. Their mouths met in a brief and electrifying kiss that sent ripples of shock waves throughout her body.

Sunny jerked back, her eyes wide.

Dash's eyes widened, and then narrowed.

Had he felt it, too?

Shaken by the entire experience, Sunny stepped backward, her heel catching on the black bag at her feet. She tipped and started to fall.

Dash's arm snaked out and caught her around the waist, bringing her back to his side where his solid form steadied her.

Her breathing coming just a little too fast, her pulse racing through her veins, Sunny blinked and pressed her palms against his bulletproof vest. "I'm okay. I just need to get out of this..." She lifted her feet, mentally cursing the high heels she'd worn for the show. If she'd been wearing sensible shoes, she might've had a chance of outrunning her captor.

Who was she kidding? The man had snuck up behind her and bagged her before she'd known what was happening. And all she'd done was to step out to find the mess hall for something different to eat.

"Miss Daye," Joe, her head bodyguard said. "I'm sorry this happened. It shouldn't have."

"Damn right it shouldn't have." She turned to the two men with the MP armbands. "I thought it was safe to move about freely inside the wire."

The military police nodded their heads. "Yes, ma'am. Normally, it is. Did you happen to see the man who grabbed you?"

She shook her head. "No."

"We don't let anyone past the gate who doesn't belong on this base," the MP said.

"Then someone on the base isn't playing the same game as the rest of you," Sunny said. "I was grabbed from behind, bagged and carried off...*inside* the wire when all I wanted to do was get a bite to eat." She shook her head. "Look. You do what you need to do to find that guy. But you should know...this isn't the first time someone has tried to take me since I landed in this country."

An older man, wearing uniform trousers, boots and buttoning a uniform jacket came running with more military police. He held out his hand. "Miss

21

Daye, we met before your show. I'm Colonel Bratton, the base commander."

She gave his hand a perfunctory shake. "I remember."

He tipped his head to the side. "Please, come with me to the command center where you and your men will be debriefed."

Still shaking inside, Sunny refused to move away from Dash's side. "I'm not going anywhere without this man."

The commander frowned. "And he is…?"

"The man who saved me. I go where he goes."

The colonel nodded. "He'll come, too. We need to get to the bottom of this matter as soon as possible."

The entourage moved as one, following the commander to a building with actual wooden sides and a wooden floor. Inside was a conference table and folding chairs enough to seat twelve.

Dash held out one of the chairs for Sunny. When she hesitated, he leaned close. "It's all right. I'm going to be in the seat beside yours."

She slipped onto the hard chair, the bare backs of her legs chilled by the cool metal.

As soon as everyone was inside and had taken their seats, the commander asked, "Can someone explain to me exactly what happened?"

Sunny drew in a deep breath and let it out slowly. "I took a walk to find the mess hall. Someone grabbed me from behind, slapped a bag over me and proceeded to carry me off."

Dash picked up from that point and rolled with it. "I ran into the man carrying Miss Daye, knocking them to the ground. I would've gone after him, but Miss Daye cried out for help. I couldn't leave her in case her captor returned."

The commander turned to the military police. "How were you alerted?"

The shorter man stepped forward. "Miss Daye's bodyguards sounded the alarm when they discovered she was missing. We were making rounds through the base when we got the radio call, not far from Miss Daye's motorhome. When we heard someone yell, we followed the sound and found Sergeant Hayes and Miss Daye. We radioed in about the abductor. The guys on perimeter are on the lookout. So far, no word."

"Sir," Paul Halverson, the man in charge of her bodyguard detail, raised his hand. "This is the second attempt to abscond with Miss Daye. Each base she's performed at has had an incident, and we have three more to go."

Colonel Bratton looked around the room. "Perhaps it's too dangerous for her to continue."

Sunny's chin lifted. "What are you saying?"

The commander's eyes narrowed. "If someone wants you bad enough, he's going to keep trying until he succeeds. Maybe it's time for you to cut your losses and go back to the States."

Before he finished his speech, Sunny was shaking her head. "Sir, I knew the risks when I signed on with the USO. I know our men and women in uniform are at equal, and more risk, every day they spend out here. It's the least I can do to provide them with a little, much-needed entertainment for all the sacrifices they make." She squared her shoulders. "I have a job to do. I'm not leaving until it's done."

Colonel Bratton stared hard at her for a long moment. "If you insist on staying, I insist on providing another level of security with someone who's a little more familiar with the state of affairs here in Afghanistan."

Sunny frowned. "I have four bodyguards. I don't need another."

The commander turned to the four men who were supposed to protect her and who'd failed. "I'm sorry, but I don't know you or your background. But I do know our Delta Forces team and trust them with my life, and I'd trust them with the lives of each member of my family." He returned his attention to Sunny. "If you insist on staying to finish out your tour, I insist on assigning at least one of my Delta Force guys to stick to you like glue."

Dash's teammate raised a hand. "Sir, I'm Delta Force Operative Michael Calhoun. I go by the call sign, Blade. I'd like to volunteer for that assignment."

Sunny shook her head, her hand reaching out to rest on Dash's arm. "If you're serious about assigning one of your men to provide my protection, I want to choose."

The commander nodded. "As long as he's Delta Force."

Her hand tightened on Dash's arm as she turned toward him. "You're Delta Force, aren't you?" she whispered to the man beside her.

He nodded and covered her hand with his. "Yes, ma'am."

"Sir, I choose Sergeant Ryan Hayes for the task."

His hand squeezed hers.

A knock sounded on the door. The man who'd identified himself as Blade opened the door a crack, poked his head out, spoke softly and then opened the door wider.

Another man in uniform with the same rank as the base commander entered and addressed Sunny first. "Miss Daye, I'm Colonel Gladson, in charge of Special Operations Forces here. Dash and Blade are part of my command." He gave a nod to each of the men then turned his attention to the base commander. "Colonel Bratton, you are responsible for the safety of everyone on this installation; however, I'm in charge of my operatives. Any taskings for my men must go through me first."

Colonel Bratton dipped his head. "Agreed. I need one of your men…" he jerked his head toward Dash, "this one, to provide additional protection to Miss Daye for the duration of her tour here in Afghanistan."

"And my men have been tasked to find the source of the human trafficking ring in this province. I can't spare a man to provide protection for one person, when there are many who will suffer in the meantime."

"I'm sorry," the base commander said. "But if Miss Daye insists on continuing her tour, she needs additional protection to ensure her safety. And based on what just happened inside my facility, the only people I really trust to handle her security are your men." He lifted his chin in Dash's direction. "Miss Daye would like to have Sergeant Hayes as her personal protection."

"Colonel Gladson," Dash jumped in, "have you considered the possibility of Miss Daye being just one more target to be acquired in the local human trafficking efforts?"

His commander's brow furrowed. "I hadn't thought about that." The Special Operations commander cupped his chin, frowning heavily. "It could be." His gaze met Sunny's, his eyes narrowing. "She'd make big bucks for their operation."

A shiver rippled down Sunny's spine. She turned to Dash. "You think they wanted to capture me to sell?"

Dash's jaw tightened. "We can't be for sure, but

there's a huge problem in this province. Women and little girls are being rounded up and sold to the highest bidders."

"If Miss Daye is a target of the trafficking ring," the special ops commander said, "then yes, we need one of my men with her at all times."

"Good," the base commander said. "In the meantime, I need to perform a complete check of the perimeter to find the breach." He nodded toward his MPs and marched for the door, stopping in front of Sunny. "By the way, the troops loved the concert. Thank you for coming." Then he was gone, followed by the MPs.

As the last MP left, six men entered, all dressed like Dash and his teammate, Blade, wearing desert camouflage uniforms, bulletproof vests and a fine layer of dust.

The man in the lead scraped the helmet off his head and plunked it on the table. "What the hell's going on? This place is lit up like a freakin' Christmas tree."

"You guys got back pretty fast," Dash commented.

The man snorted. "Fast until we hit the gate and got the third degree from a heavy contingent of guards. They almost didn't let us bring the truck full of women and children inside the gate." His gaze shifted from Dash to Blade, and then finally to their special operations commander. "Anyone want to tell me what's going on?"

The colonel's lips twisted. He nodded toward the table where Sunny sat.

She turned to fully face the men who'd entered. Their eyes widened.

"Holy shit. You're Sunny Daye." The lead man exclaimed.

Sunny chuckled. "Yes, I am."

The man's eyes narrowed, and his gaze shot to Dash. "Please tell me our man Dash didn't make you give him a full concert for him alone."

Sunny's glance shot to Dash. "No, he didn't."

The man's eyes widened. "He didn't try to sneak into your quarters or hold you hostage, did he?"

Sunny laughed. "No, as a matter of fact, he saved me from being abducted by somebody else."

The man's brow twisted. "What the hell? Is that why the guards are all in a knot and this place is lit up?"

Dash nodded. "I stopped the abduction but didn't catch the guy who did it."

The soldier raked a hand through his short hair. "No wonder they gave us the third degree coming through the gate."

"We don't know who he was or how he got on the base," Dash said. "We need to find the guy who tried to take off with Miss Daye."

The soldier frowned. "Is it me or is it too much of a coincidence that the man we were tasked to catch left the human auction early and Miss Daye's abduction happened shortly after?"

"The connection did cross our minds," the Special Operations commander said. "That's why the base commander insisted on putting one of our guys on Miss Daye's security detail until her tour is complete and she leaves Afghanistan."

Dash waved a hand toward the man in front of the others. "Miss Daye, this is Rucker Sloan, our team lead."

Sunny pushed back her chair, ready to stand.

The man held up a hand. "Don't get up." He closed the distance between them and held out a hand. "I love your music, Miss Daye. It's a pleasure to meet you."

Still seated, her cheeks heated as she shook his hand. "The pleasure is mine."

One by one, Dash introduced her to his team.

"The big guy with the bulky shoulders is Craig Bullington. We call him Bull."

Bull stepped forward and took her hand in a surprisingly gentle grip. "Miss Daye."

She smiled. "Do I call you Craig or Bull?"

He grinned. "You can call me anything you want."

"The wiry guy behind Bull is Dawg, aka Doug Masters. He's the best shot on the team."

The man stepped forward. "Pleasure."

Sunny shook his hand. "The best shot? Are you a sniper?"

He held up the high-powered rifle with a scope attached. "Yes, ma'am."

"You've met Blade." Dash nodded toward his teammate. "The man is an expert knife thrower."

"Aren't knives old school?" she asked.

"Not when silence is key to an operation," Blade said, then winked.

Sunny nodded. "I guess so."

Dash waved to a tall man with green eyes. "Sean McDaniels."

"Most folks call me Mac," McDaniels said.

"Nice to meet you, Mac," Sunny said.

"Tank, come say hello to Miss Daye." Dash waved a big guy over from where he perched near the door.

Tank frowned and pushed his way through the others.

"Miss Daye, this is John Sanders."

She shook the man's hand with a smile. "Why do they call you Tank?"

The big guy shrugged.

A handsome man with black hair and gray eyes stepped up beside Tank and draped an arm over his shoulder. "We call him Tank because he's as graceful as an M1 Abrams tank." He held out his hand. "Lance Rankin at your service."

She took Lance's hand briefly.

When she released his hand, he grinned. "I can't believe I'm actually talking with Sunny Daye. Please, ma'am, I'd be honored to volunteer my services to protect you."

Blade snorted. "Dash got that lucky assignment."

"It's a pleasure to meet all of you," Sunny said. "Since Dash saved me, I'm going to stick with him until I leave the country." Her brow dipped. "What was it you said about a truckload of women and children?"

Rucker shook his head. "We just got back from a mission to find the source of the human trafficking in the area. We caught them in the act of auctioning off women and children."

Sunny's heart squeezed hard in her chest. She knew human trafficking was a problem worldwide, but she'd never actually come that close to seeing it happen. "That's awful." She turned to Dash. "You think these people were trying to capture me to sell to their sleezy buyers?"

Dash shrugged. "It's possible."

"The bad news is," Rucker said, "we didn't catch the man who's been negotiating the deals. He left the auction before we could spring the trap."

"So, he's still out there, brokering humans?" Sunny shivered.

"He is." Rucker frowned and turned to Dash. "So, how is it you got the assignment to protect Miss Daye?"

Dash tipped his head toward Sunny. "The base

commander insisted she either add a more qualified man to her security team or go home."

"Don't celebrities come with their own body-guards?" Rucker asked.

Dash's lips pressed into a tight line. "She had four, and that guy still got to her. What's going to happen to the women and children now?"

"They're erecting a tent for them to sleep in for the night. From what I understand, they're scrounging as many cots and blankets as they can find. Tomorrow, our intel people will be working with them to see if they can glean any information about the man responsible for the trade of humans. They'll eventually be moved to a refugee contain-ment center to be processed and returned home, if possible."

Sunny pressed a hand to her chest. "How horrible to be treated like cattle. Those women and children must be terrified. Is there anything me or my people can do to ease their plight?"

The Special Operations commander gave her a brief smile. "Not unless you have some blankets and pillows you can spare."

"I'll talk with my people." Glad to have something productive to do, Sunny pushed away from the table and stood. She was halfway to the door when the commander's voice stopped her.

"Miss Daye, don't forget. You're going to have a shadow in our man, Dash."

She frowned. "I hate to take him away from more important duties than following me around. I'd rather he spent his time finding the man responsible for this travesty of human trafficking."

"Ma'am, Dash is good at what he does," the colonel said. "His methods may be unorthodox at times, but his intentions are good, and he's effective. If the man in charge of human trafficking in this area was after you for the same financial gain as he was with the women and children rescued tonight, you might be the key to capturing this guy."

Sunny nodded. "Then I won't feel so bad taking your soldier away from his normal duties."

The commander gave her a brief smile. "Don't worry. We'll be in close contact with Dash at all times, and on call, should you need the entire team to come to your aid if anything goes south."

As Sunny walked the gauntlet of broad-shouldered, tough-looking Delta Force team soldiers, she shook hands and thanked them for their service. She paused at the door and turned to wait for Dash.

"Dude," Tank said, clapping a hand on Dash's shoulder. "Let me know if you need someone to give you a break. I would gladly take your place."

"I've already volunteered, and was shot down," Blade said. "She wants Dash. Although what she sees in him, I don't know."

"Dumb ass," Lance said. "Dash saved her from being abducted. Where were you?"

Blade sighed. "Obviously, in the wrong place at the wrong time."

Sunny smothered a grin as Dash's teammates all clapped him on the back and congratulated him.

His gaze met hers.

A shiver of awareness, and maybe anticipation, rippled across her body. This man was unlike any she'd met in the music industry, including her bodyguards.

Dash was a man's man, strong, broad-shouldered, tough as nails. A man who didn't run from a gunfight but ran into it.

Sunny felt a stab of guilt for taking him away from his team and their important mission. She assuaged her guilt with the idea that she, too, was a target. By keeping Dash with her, they might find the human trafficker.

Having the handsome soldier at her side wouldn't be a hardship. Not in the least.

CHAPTER 3

AFTER RUNNING through the line of his teammates punching his shoulders, slapping him on the back and making rude comments, Dash followed Sunny out of the building, glad to get out into the cool night air.

Sunny stood with her four bodyguards, talking in hushed tones. She glanced up and smiled at him as he joined them.

"Guys, this is Ryan Hayes. He goes by Dash. He'll be with me 24/7 until I leave Afghanistan."

As Sunny introduced each one by name, Dash shook hands.

They seemed nice enough and appeared in good shape. Why the hell had they let someone get to their client?

Dash was glad Sunny had chosen him as her own personal Delta Force protector. He vowed to do a better job keeping track of her. He understood that being in charge of her safety was a lot of responsibility.

As a celebrity, even in the States, she probably needed around the clock security. In a foreign country, where the enemy wanted to kill all Americans, she was even more of a target. The only consolation was that they probably didn't want to kill her. She'd be worth a whole lot more alive to sell to the highest bidder. Some rich oil tycoon might want his own personal singer/songwriter to add to his harem.

Given the massive amount of oil money available in the Middle East, she could generate a significant sum of cash for whomever captured and sold her.

All the more reason for the human trafficker to try again.

Feeling the weight of his responsibilities bearing down on his shoulders, he moved closer to Sunny Daye.

"Where to?" he asked.

"I'd like to get back to my people to see if we can do anything to help the women and children who've been displaced." She glanced at the long row of tent quarters. "I'm not sure exactly how to get back to our vehicles."

Dash chuckled. "The base isn't that big. I'm sure we can figure this out." He cupped her elbow in his palm and guided her in the direction he remembered seeing the USO vans and trucks when they'd flown back in the helicopters. Soon, they emerged from a row of buildings to find the trucks and vans with the large USO lettering on their sides.

Back in familiar territory, Sunny led the way to one of the motorhomes and knocked on the door.

A man answered. His eyes widened, and he reached for her hands. "Please, Sunny, come in."

Sunny climbed the steps into the motorhome.

Dash remained on the ground.

She turned. "You, too. You heard the base commander. I'm not allowed to go anywhere without you."

He nodded and followed her into the unit. Inside, the motorhome was set up like a small apartment with a fully-equipped kitchen, a comfortable living room and hallway, leading to the rear where Dash assumed was a bathroom and bedroom.

"Lloyd, this is Dash—or rather, Ryan Hayes." She gave him a crooked smile. "The base commander assigned him to me as an addition to my security detail." She turned to Dash. "This is Lloyd Pendleton, the USO coordinator for this tour."

Lloyd frowned. "I don't understand. You already have four bodyguards."

Her lips firmed. "And yet, someone was able to get past them to bag me and carry me off without one of them noticing. If not for Dash, who knows where I'd be right now?"

Lloyd held out his hand to Dash, his eyes narrowing. "Hayes." He gave a brief nod. "What qualifications do you have to make you a better fit to provide for Miss Daye's safety than her four bodyguards?"

Dash took the man's hand in a brief, yet bone-crunching shake. "Sir, bodyguards in the States might be sufficient. However, in this theater of operations, you might be dealing with the Taliban, indigenous people who will do anything for money to feed their families and mercenary contractors, who would rather steal money from the government than do the right thing. Stateside bodyguards might not be as effective against them."

"And you will be?" Lloyd challenged, tugging on his hand.

"I'll do my best, sir." Dash released the man.

"Good." Lloyd rubbed his right hand with his left. "Miss Daye is our main attraction. I'd hate to lose her."

"And I'd hate to disappoint the troops," Sunny added. "They work hard. They deserve a little entertainment."

Lloyd faced Sunny. "Are you sure you want to continue this tour? Even though you're the main attraction, if it's not safe, maybe we should put you on the first plane home."

Sunny was already shaking her head. "I signed on, knowing the risks. The least I can do is see it through. There are a lot of troops out there who've risked their lives for us. I'm not going to leave at the first sign of trouble. They don't have that option."

"Yeah, but is it worth risking your life when you're an actual target?" Lloyd asked. "This isn't the first sign of trouble."

"I know," she said.

"Hell, you had just barely gotten off the plane in Kabul when someone tried to snag you." Lloyd shook his head. "It was a good thing you had the wherewithal to clobber the guy with your carryon bag." Lloyd grinned. "I'd have given my full month's salary to have seen that."

"Sir," Dash interrupted, "would it be better to fly Miss Daye to her next location? Traveling by road in Afghanistan is iffy at best, dangerous at its worst."

Lloyd's grin sobered. "I understand, but we don't have it in our budget to fly our people around. Besides, the Army is providing a security detail for our convoy."

"And you think it's sufficient?" Dash asked.

"So far." Lloyd glanced at Sunny. "She was attacked here in the compound. I'd say the security on the base is lax if someone was able to get inside and grab Miss Daye."

"I can't argue with you there," Dash said.

Again, Lloyd glanced toward Sunny then nodded toward the door. "Miss Daye, you might want to get some sleep in what's left of the night. We leave first thing in the morning.

He nodded toward Dash. "In the meantime, where do you want him to sleep?"

"I don't need sleep," Dash said.

"You'll need it if you want to keep up with Miss Daye." Lloyd walked with Sunny and Dash to the door.

"One other thing," Sunny said.

"Yes, Miss Daye."

"The Deltas brought in a truckload of women and children who'd been targeted for human trafficking. They were being auctioned as the Deltas closed in on them. Are there any blankets or pillows we can spare to give to those poor women and children. They have nothing but the clothes on their backs. They need somewhere safe and warm to sleep while they're waiting to be reunited with their families."

"I'm sure we can come up with some items," Llyod said. "I think there are spare blankets and pillows in the closets. Let's check it out. I'm sure I have two blankets and some pillows in my unit. We can check with the other trailers and see what we can find."

Sunny glanced down at the outfit she'd performed in. "I need to grab something from my quarters before I go."

Dash and her bodyguards, followed Sunny to her motorhome and waited outside while she threw a loose cape over her shoulders that covered her from neck to toe, hiding her sequined miniskirt and sparkly tank top.

In the next fifteen minutes, Lloyd, Sunny, Dash and the bodyguards knocked on the motorhomes, woke their occupants and collected eleven blankets and as many pillows.

"We'll deliver these to the refugees," Lloyd said.

Sunny shook her head. "I'm going with you," she said. "I can't imagine what those women and children felt like. I was lucky. I wasn't taken far from familiar surroundings. Dash saved me before I was subjected to the humiliation of being auctioned."

"I'm not sure they'll let you into the tent," Dash said.

Sunny's lips thinned. "Whether or not they let us in, we're carrying these items to those people. I'm sure they need whatever comfort they can get."

Dash crossed his arms over his chest and nodded. "As you wish."

"Let me get the camera crew," Lloyd said. "This would be a good opportunity to get some PR."

"I don't need the PR," Sunny said. "I just want to help those women and children."

"I understand," Lloyd said. "But the USO could use the PR. So, if you don't mind, I'd like to record you helping the people of Afghanistan. If we get footage of the troops assisting as well, then all the better. Good PR all around."

Sunny sighed. "All right. I'll agree with that. But I'd rather have more video of the troops helping out than me."

Lloyd grinned. "Deal."

With her arms filled with blankets and pillows, Sunny Daye marched across the compound to the tent that had been erected for the victims who'd been rescued earlier.

Dash followed, carrying blankets and pillows as well. He didn't like that his hands were full. He'd have to drop everything, if he had a need to pull his rifle up to firing position or grab his handgun from the holster at his side. But the woman he was protecting had insisted that they help others. He admired her dedication to serve and assist those in need.

A perimeter had been set up around the tent with soldiers stationed in a circle, ten yards out with fifty feet between each. They were there to protect the women from intruders and to keep the women and children confined to their tent and the immediate vicinity.

After each burden was inspected thoroughly, they were allowed to go inside the tent. The videographer entered first and recorded the event.

Women and children sat on cots or huddled on the ground, shivering in the cool night air. Some were swaddled in sleeping bags they'd been provided, sharing warmth with each other.

They were happy to receive the blankets and pillows Sunny and her crew provided.

Children who were awake crowded around Sunny's legs, eager to be close to the woman with the golden hair. She knelt beside them, allowing them to touch her long, silky tresses. Sunny spoke softly to each of them.

They couldn't understand a word she said, but it was the way she spoke in a soothing tone that made them smile and want to hold her hand.

When all the blankets and pillows had been distributed, Lloyd leaned close to Sunny. "You did good."

She sighed, looking at the misery all around her. "I did what any decent human being would have done."

A small child approached her and took her hand, tears streaming down her face.

Sunny sat on the ground beside her, pulling the child into her arms. Speaking softly, she tried to sooth the little one's sorrow. When the little girl's tears continued, Sunny started to sing a sweet lullaby, rocking the child in her arms.

As she sang, the voices in the tent hushed as everyone listened to the angelic sound.

Sunny's song tugged at Dash's heart. He knew her music from the radio, but hearing it in person, in such a sweet acapella, made it that much more personal and poignant.

Dash finally understood the magic of Sunny Daye. He could hear the love and longing in the sweet notes. Her tone was clear and pure, and she sang as if it came straight from her heart.

The child snuggled against her and soon fell asleep.

After repeating the song several times, Sunny glanced up. "I hate to leave her."

One of the women reached out, took the child from Sunny's arms and wrapped her in a blanket as if she were her own.

Dash helped Sunny to her feet. "Come on. We need to let them sleep. You need to get some sleep, too."

She nodded. "You need your sleep, as well. You must be exhausted."

He gave her a crooked grin as they walked out of the tent into the starlit night. "I'm not the one who put on a show tonight, and then got kidnapped."

He cupped her elbow and led her across the compound back to the line of trucks, vans and motorhomes.

Her bodyguards fell into step behind them.

When they arrived at her motorhome, she started to reach for the door handle.

Dash touched her arm. "Let me go first."

While Sunny waited at the foot of the steps, Dash entered the motorhome. He checked all the rooms, the closets and storage areas, searching for intruders. His check only took moments, and he was back at the door, holding it open. "All clear. You can come in."

She entered, stifling a yawn.

When he started for the door, she stopped him

with a hand on his shoulder. "Wait. Where are you going?"

"While you sleep, I'll be outside, guarding your place."

"That won't be necessary," she said.

His lips pressed into a thin line. "It will be necessary."

She shook her head. "My bodyguards take turns. Two stay awake while the other two sleep. Then they swap with the other two. That way, everyone gets some sleep." She looked around the interior of the unit. "If you don't mind, I'd prefer you stay inside. Don't worry. The bodyguards stand on each end of the trailer at opposite corners."

"Where do your bodyguards sleep?" Dash asked.

"They have their own small trailer where they take turns sleeping in the bunks."

"I really don't mind standing guard outside."

Sunny's lips pressed together. "Mr. Hayes, are you afraid of me?"

Dash's eyes widened. "Of course not." If he was truthful, he was afraid of himself. Or more to the point, he was afraid of being alone with Sunny.

"I'd feel more comfortable if you were someplace, that if I called out, you would hear me." Her glance shot to one of the windows that was covered with blinds. "I don't think you would hear me if you were outside."

"Fair enough," Dash said.

"With the bodyguards standing guard outside, you can get some sleep as well." Sunny tipped her chin toward the sofa. "The couch opens out into a queen-sized bed."

Dash shook his head. "If it's all right with you, I'll sleep on the couch, without extending the bed."

"Suit yourself." As she walked toward the back of the unit, she kicked off her shoes and padded away barefooted. She let the cape she'd worn to the tent fall to the ground. "Don't judge me," she said, casting a glance over her shoulder. "I'll pick these up in the morning."

Oh, he was judging all right. The woman had legs from her toes all the way up to her chin, and they were gorgeous. The miniskirt did nothing but emphasize how long and slender her legs were.

When she reached the door to her room, she turned back. "There's food in the refrigerator. Help yourself. I'm leaving this door open so I can hear you and you can hear me." Then she disappeared for a few minutes. The sound of a shower made Dash tense.

He could imagine Sunny naked, standing beneath the spray. The water didn't stay on long. A few minutes later, the woman occupying his carnal thoughts appeared in baby doll pajama shorts and a tank top.

Sunny had pulled her hair up into a messy bun on top of her head using an elastic band. Loose blond strands hung down around her neck, making Dash want to brush them back from her face and tuck them behind her ears. Or better yet, pull the elastic band from her hair and let her hair fall down around her shoulders again. He longed to run his hands through it.

He paced the living room, unable to sit due to the tightness of his trousers. Shrugging out of his bullet-proof vest, he set it down beside the door, next to his rifle. He pulled the handgun out of the holster on his hip and laid it on the countertop.

Dash tried to focus on anything but the woman in the next room. A woman whose legs he could imagine wrapped around his waist as he drove deep inside of her.

Holy shit. What was he thinking?

They'd only just met.

She was a celebrity.

He was just a grunt.

They occupied two completely different worlds. It wasn't like they'd ever come together as a couple. The only thing that could possibly happen between them was a short fling. And by short, it would be the amount of time until she finished her tour and left Afghanistan. Then Sunny would go her way, while Dash stayed in Afghanistan, fighting a foe he couldn't always see. Even if he redeployed back to Fort Hood, Texas, he wouldn't see her. She'd be on tour, gone twelve months out of the year.

Despite all the cons, she'd sparked a huge amount of desire in Dash's loins in the few short hours he'd known her.

Not only was she beautiful, she really cared enough about strangers to donate blankets and pillows to women and children in need. And she sang like an angel and had a body that could tempt the devil out of any man.

Dash was mesmerized by her. For the next fifteen minutes he paced, his adrenaline racing through his veins. From saving Sunny to watching her strut past the open door in her baby doll pajamas, he couldn't slow his wildly beating heart. Blood pumped hard and fast through his veins. Hard and fast like he'd like to take her, sliding deep inside her warm wetness.

Damn. What was he thinking? They were in a war zone. Fraternizing with anyone in a war zone would get you sent back to the states ASAP, if it didn't get him court-martialed first. Anything he might want to do with or to Miss Daye would be completely against the rules.

A slow smile slid across his face. Dash ignored rules when they didn't make sense, or he didn't care for them. He'd found it better to act first and beg forgiveness later. As long as the woman was willing.

CHAPTER 4

DASH TURNED AWAY from the bedroom and walked toward the front of the motorhome, struggling to get a grip on his desires. When he turned back to the bedroom, he spotted Sunny. She stood in the hallway at the end of the living room, wearing nothing but those darned baby doll pajamas in a pale powder blue. They were nearly sheer.

Dash could see the rosy tips of her nipples through the filmy fabric.

She frowned. "Can't sleep either?"

He shook his head. Oh, hell no. Not with her lying in the bed in the other room wearing that...that tempting cotton candy nightwear.

Of course, he didn't say that out loud, but his body screamed it.

"Me either," she said. "Every time I close my eyes, I feel like I'm in the pitch-black of that body bag. I can only imagine what might have happened if you hadn't come along and saved me."

"You're a smart woman," he said. "You'd have figured out a way to escape."

"Do you mind if I keep you company?" she asked.

His lips quirked upward. "It's your place."

She nodded and crossed to the couch, sat and folded her legs beneath her and pulled a pillow across her chest.

She patted the cushion beside her. "Come sit with me."

When he didn't move, she added, "Please."

He sat at the far end of the couch, which wasn't very far, since the seating was only half the size of a normal sofa. All he had to do was move his leg a little and it would touch her thigh.

"Tell me about yourself," Sunny said. "Talk to me, and maybe I'll get sleepy."

"I don't have much to tell," he hedged, not really wanting to talk about himself when it was her he'd rather know more about.

"I'm sure you're a very interesting person."

"Not really," he said.

Her lips twisted. "I see I'm going to have to pull it out of you."

"Seriously," he said. "There's not much to tell."

She tightened her hold on the pillow. "We can start with what I do know. You're Delta Force,

50

deployed to Afghanistan. The training must have been pretty hard to achieve Delta Force status."

He shrugged. "It was okay."

She snorted. "And you're a smartass as well as a badass. What made you try out for Delta Force?"

"I like the challenge," he said.

"What made you join the Army?" she asked.

He looked away. "I didn't have anything better to do."

"Are you married?" she asked.

"Ha," he said. "Not hardly." What woman wanted a part-time husband? Some thought they did, until they tried it. Those marriages didn't last long.

"Do you have any family back home?" she continued.

"A sister. Briana." He loved his sister.

"Are you close?"

Dash nodded. "We are. She's the only family I have left."

Sunny reached out to touch his arm. "I'm sorry."

"Don't be. We look out for each other," he said. "That's what counts."

"Yes, it does. And at least you do have each other." She gave him a wistful smile. "Does she look like you?"

"No, thank God. She's much better looking."

"Where did you two grow up?"

"Outside of Chicago."

"What was it like to be a younger version of Ryan Hayes, before you became Dash?"

He shrugged. "Busy. Always camping, hiking, and fishing with my Dad. He instilled in me a love of the outdoors."

"And here we are in the great outdoors of Afghanistan. When you were a teen, did you picture yourself here?"

He nodded. "I always knew I'd go into the military." His eyes narrowed. "Enough about me. What about you?"

Her lips twisted into a wry grin. "What about me?"

"How old were you when you started singing professionally?" he asked.

She glanced away. "Thirteen. I auditioned for one of those talent programs on television. I was selected and made it all the way to the finale."

"And you won," he said. "Thirteen. Wow. That's awful young to be subjected to the cutthroat performance industry. How long ago was that?"

She glanced down at her hands. "Fourteen years."

Dash did the math. That would put Sunny at twenty-seven years old. "How old were you when you earned your first double platinum record?"

She sighed. "I was eighteen, had the world in front of me, and was well on the way to having all my dreams come true."

He tilted his head as he studied her profile. "You

say that as if you realize it wasn't all it was cracked up to be."

She shrugged. "I guess it wasn't all I thought it would be. It was a little more difficult."

"Was that when you met your partner?"

Sunny nodded. "Just past my eighteenth birthday, my agent teamed me with Justin Snow for a duet. That song sold so many copies, my agent decided Justin and I made a good team. We recorded an entire album together."

"You were together for twelve years…?" Dash asked.

"Eleven," she said.

"I take it you two were really close," Dash said. "Did you ever consider marrying?"

She shook her head. "I kept waiting for him to ask." Her mouth turned up on one corner. "He never did. I reached the point where I was ready to give him an ultimatum. Either we marry, or we end the partnership. I needed to move on."

Dash's brows rose.

Sunny snorted softly. "What? The tabloids didn't get hold of that news?"

He lifted a shoulder. "If they did, I wouldn't have known. I don't read the tabloids."

"Well, it didn't matter anyway," she said staring at the wall in front of her.

"Why's that?" he asked softly.

"We were on the road between stops on our tour

when we got into a heated argument. I had them stop the bus, got off and climbed into one of the equipment vans. We were in the vehicle behind the motorhome Justin was in, when a vehicle crossed the median and hit the motorhome head-on. We watched as it ran off the road and rolled several times before it came to a stop upside down in a small lake. Nobody but the driver was wearing a seatbelt inside the motorhome. By the time we got to the vehicle, it had sunk below the surface and was completely submerged."

"That had to be a pretty traumatic event for you."

She nodded. "It was winter. The water was icy cold. We all dove in, at least once, but we couldn't get to the door to let anyone out. The only one who made it out was the driver. He'd been the only one wearing a seatbelt and wasn't thrown all over the place. Justin and three members of the band were left in that motorhome, and all of them died."

"Let me guess," Dash said. "You've been living with survivor's guilt ever since."

Sunny drew in a deep breath and let it out slowly. "I was supposed to be in that motorhome. If I had been, I would have been dead, along with Justin and the band. Instead, I watched it all happen right there in front of me. No matter how hard I tried, I couldn't get into that RV to save them."

"Why did you join the USO?" Dash asked.

She stared down at her hands. "After nine years of

singing as a couple, I didn't know how to sing alone." Her gaze met his. "The USO came to me and asked if I'd be interested in entertaining the troops for a couple of months. I saw it as a way to escape." She lifted her shoulders. "So, here I am."

Dash shook his head. "Escape? Here? Are you sure you weren't punishing yourself for surviving?"

Sunny's head shot up, and she stared at him. "What do you mean?"

"You joined the USO, came to a war-torn country where you put yourself at risk. Sounds to me like you were punishing yourself for living when the others had died."

For a long moment, she stared at him.

He met her gaze without flinching. He supposed he'd hit a nerve.

Finally, she glanced away. "Maybe you're right. Maybe I am punishing myself for living when Justin hadn't."

"Had he lived, you were about to tell him you were breaking up the team anyway," he pointed out.

"Yes, I would've ended the duo, but I didn't wish him dead because he didn't want to marry me."

"The man must've been blind."

Her gaze shot to his. "Why do you say that?"

"I mean, look at you." He waved a hand, encompassing all of her. "You're beautiful."

"So are a million other women," she shot back at him. "I guess I'd assumed that he would eventually marry me. After nine years, I gave up hope. We really wanted different things. I wanted a home and family. He wanted to be on the road, touring. He lived for the audience and soaked up the attention of all the gorgeous women who fawned over him at every stop. I was ready to find normalcy in an abnormal environment."

"Like I said," Dash said. "The man must've been blind."

"What about you and marriage?" she asked. "You said you aren't married. But have you ever been? Did you get divorced?"

"Never married. Never divorced."

"Were you like Justin and never wanted to get married?"

He shook his head. "I had a happy childhood with loving parents. They stayed home and participated in all of our sporting events, school plays and everything else that made up childhood."

Her brow wrinkled. "You'd think that would make you want to marry and have a family."

"I didn't want to have a family, unless I could do it right. With Delta Force, being away from home is more the norm than being at home. I'd miss all the firsts with my kids. First birthday, first steps, first time she rides a bike, first time he throws a football. I couldn't do it."

"You talk about kids... What about a relationship

without children? Didn't you ever want to find someone to love?"

He nodded, and then shook his head. "What kind of life would that be for a woman? She'd be alone for most of the year, wondering when I'd come home, and if it would be in a body bag. There aren't many women who can tolerate the long absences."

"You'd think they'd understand that when they signed on to marry a Delta Force soldier," Sunny said.

"It's all love and happiness for the first few months until the Delta is deployed with an indefinite return date. We can be gone for a few weeks up to a year, or more, at a time. That leaves the woman alone for all that time. Not everyone is good at being alone. Especially when small children are involved. It really takes two to parent."

Sunny frowned. "No, it takes a strong woman to hold down the fort while her husband is deployed, fighting for his life, or for the lives of his teammates."

"Exactly," Dash said.

"Tell me about your sister." Sunny smiled. "Is she in the military, too?"

He laughed. "Oh, hell no. But get this...she's in love with a buddy of mine from one of the other Delta Force teams."

"Is she strong enough to handle being without her man for extended periods?" Sunny asked.

"In Briana's case, she doesn't have to worry about

that. Rafe, her fiancé, left the military and took a job with a security company up in Montana. He's working as an agent for Hank Patterson's Brotherhood Protectors. His company provides security and assistance using former military special forces men and women."

"So, he'll be home more than he's away." Sunny smiled. again. "That'll be better for their relationship."

Dash nodded. "He still has assignments, but they're mostly stateside. And my sister loves to work and take care of children placed in the foster system. She knows how to keep busy. It's good that he gave up the military before committing to my sister. Being Delta Force doesn't lend itself to marriage."

Sunny's brow furrowed. "Or is it just that you don't want to marry, don't want a family and don't want to commit, and Delta Force is just a good excuse to play the field?"

His jaw hardened. "Maybe I don't want to commit because I don't want to put a woman through what she'd have to deal with."

"Or maybe you haven't found a woman who is strong enough to handle being alone for long stretches of time."

He dipped his head. "You have a point."

"What about your sister?" Sunny asked.

Dash laughed. "I'm not marrying my sister."

"No, that's not what I meant." Sunny frowned. "What about her and the Delta she's falling in love with? He might not be active Delta, but his work as a security agent might take him away for long stretches of time."

"My sister is a badass. She can handle it."

Sunny cocked an eyebrow. "And you think she's the only woman who's tough enough to handle it?"

Dash shrugged. He didn't like being put on the spot like this.

"You know what I think?" she said waggling her eyebrows.

He rolled his eyes. "I'm afraid to ask."

"I think you're selling yourself short." She lifted her chin. "If marriage and a family is what you really want, you should find that woman who could handle it and make it happen."

"You know what I think?" Dash echoed.

Her eyes narrowed. "What?"

Dash leaned forward and touched the tip of her nose. "That you need to go to sleep." Then he tucked a strand of her hair behind her ear, leaned closer and pressed his lips to hers.

It happened so fast he didn't have time to think. He acted on an urge that was as natural as breathing.

The fact that she kissed him back hit him square in the gut.

Shocked by his action and her reaction, he leaned back, his gaze locking with hers for a long moment.

She raised her hand to touch her lips. "Why did you do that?"

"I don't know," he said. "It seemed right at the moment." His brow descended. "But if you ask me to apologize, I'm afraid I can't do that?"

"Why?"

His thoughts lightened as the truth shone through. He smiled. "Because I liked it too much to be sorry I did it."

"Well, you shouldn't have done it," she said, her voice breathy.

He chuckled. "It's too late. I already did."

She sat up straighter, her eyebrows coming together over the bridge of her nose. "We should probably get a few things straight."

"Really?" He crossed his arms over his chest. "What things?"

"What I tell all the men who provide security services for me."

"And what is it you tell them?" he asked.

"Number one," she said raising her index finger. "Hands off."

He shook his head. "Broke that rule already. Kinda had to in order to pull you out of that body bag. What else have you got?" He wanted to laugh at her attempt to keep them on neutral footing, when it was obvious she was as attracted to him as he was to her.

"Two." She held up two fingers, and then touched her lips with them, her eyes glazing over. "No...kissing."

Dash's grin grew broader. "Once again, I've broken that rule as well. Any more rules I should be aware of?"

She nodded, and her voice dropped to little more than a whisper. "No falling in love with the talent."

His breath caught in his throat as he stared hard at the woman sitting across from him.

Love?

He'd sworn off love the moment he'd entered Delta Force. Sharing a motorhome with this amazing singer wouldn't make him rethink his stance on no relationships until he left the force.

She held up her hands, the pillow falling to her lap, exposing her semi-sheer pajama top. Her nipples grew tight in the cool air, forming twin peaks beneath the powder blue flimsy fabric.

Dash's groin tightened to the point he was uncomfortable sitting. He drew in a deep breath and let it out slowly. "Maybe I have a few rules, too."

CHAPTER 5

"RULES?" Sunny's voice squeaked. Then in a more measured tone, she said, "Really? Like what?"

He held up his index finger. "One: never wear those night clothes unless you want me to touch you."

She shivered at the hot glance he ran over her body and across her exposed knees. Sunny gulped back a rush of desire that stunned her and made her all shivery inside. "That goes against my rule number one of *Don't touch*."

"Yes, and no. If you don't wear that, I won't be as tempted to touch. If you wear that, I'll assume you want me to touch you."

Her shoulders straightened. Hell, she'd show up naked and see what he had to say about that.

His brow creased. "On second thought, I don't think it's the nightclothes. You have a way of making a man want to touch you. I'll just have to retain focus on the mission and ignore my baser instincts."

"And that's possible?" She raised a single eyebrow. "You just kissed me...unprovoked."

"Yeah, but you kissed me back," he said with a grin.

She straightened and lifted her chin. "I did not."

"Want me to do it again to test the theory?" He leaned forward, his face so close it wouldn't take much for their lips to meet.

She swayed toward him, and her lips touched his. The connection sent a jolt of electricity through her.

He gathered her to him, his arms tightening around her, pressing her breasts to his chest.

Sunny couldn't fight the heat that overwhelmed her and made her want to be even closer. She surrendered to his mouth, opening to let him sweep past her teeth to caress her tongue.

Sweet heaven, he tasted so good and felt even better. His hands in her hair, her body pressed to his sparked more than desire. It generated a Tsunami of feelings she'd never felt before. Pure, unadulterated lust. She wanted to take him into her, there on the couch. Now.

When he lifted his head, she strained to follow him, only to be left looking up into his dancing eyes.

He brushed his thumb across her cheek. "My point is proven."

Damn him.

She leaned away from him. "You've proven nothing."

He tightened his arms around her back, bringing her close again. "Want to go for round three?"

"No," she whispered, her gaze on his lips, her desire swelling again. Yes, she wanted to go for round three with the Delta. No, she couldn't tell him that. Not and keep the ball in her court.

She almost laughed out loud at herself. Her court? Ha! He had all the advantage with his hunky body, his strong hands and those lips that set her entire being on fire.

She cleared her throat and pushed her hands against his chest. "That was number one. Do you have any more rules?"

He nodded. "Two: If you want to kiss me, all you have to do is ask."

"That goes against my *No Kissing* rule."

"Only if you sneak one in on me." He winked. "I'm not saying I'll refuse you, but a guy likes to know when his woman wants him."

"I don't—"

Dash pressed a finger to her lips. "Shh. Now, don't lie. It doesn't look good on an angel."

She frowned. "I'm not an angel."

"You look and sound like one." He brushed his thumb across her cheek again. "Get some sleep."

She glanced toward the darkened bedroom and back up at him. She didn't want to return to her nightmares. "Do you mind if I stay here until I go to sleep?"

"Again," he waved his hand out to the side, "it's your place."

Sunny pulled her legs back beneath her, still clutching the pillow to her chest. She curled up in the corner of the couch, taking up less space than most people would and closed her eyes.

Dash headed for the back of the motorhome, grabbed a blanket from the bed and returned to cover Sunny's legs.

"You can sit on the couch," she said. "I don't bite. Not much, anyway."

"I will when I get tired," he assured her.

She propped one eye open. "Will it help if I sing a lullaby?"

He shook his head. "I'm not a child."

"You're never too old for a lullaby," she said with a yawn.

"Go to sleep, Sunny."

Her eyelids drooped and closed, and her breathing became deeper until most thoughts and worries faded into the abyss of sleep. The image of Dash standing in her motor coach was the last one on her mind, calming at the same time as it excited her.

. . .

DASH PACED the living room and down the hallway to the bedroom and back. What had he gotten himself into?

This woman was more than just a security assignment. She was a reminder of everything he missed in his life.

Dash and his sister, Briana, had experienced the storybook family life with a mother and father to come home to. His reluctance to start a family of his own was based on that exact life. He didn't want to subject a wife and children to anything less than what he'd had growing up.

His parents had set the bar, and he wanted to live up to it. If he couldn't provide that now, then he wouldn't marry and have children until he could. It wouldn't be fair to a women to get her pregnant and leave her to shoulder the entire burden of raising a child or children.

As a Delta Force operative, he wouldn't be there to provide his share of parenting. He didn't blame the women who divorced his teammates. They wanted men who were partners in raising a family. Delta Force soldiers couldn't always be there. They were married to the military, and that job came first.

Bottom line, he hadn't married because he couldn't give a woman and children the storybook family he'd been blessed to have.

When, and if, he decided to marry and have children, he'd have to make that tough decision to give up the military and Delta Force, a team of men he'd grown to love like brothers.

And when he did marry, he wanted a woman as kind and caring as Sunny. Hell, he'd love that woman to be Sunny.

Who was he kidding? Sunny wouldn't be interested in a man like him. She was a celebrity. She was so far out of his league he couldn't begin to compete with all the men she had to choose from.

He was there to protect her life, not to become a part of it.

Eventually, he settled on the couch beside her, kicked his feet up on an ottoman and leaned his head back. He'd rest his eyes a little. It wouldn't be long before the caravan of coaches had to leave for their next stop. He'd need to keep awake and alert on the move.

Dash must have fallen asleep. When he woke, a warm body was snuggled up against him, an arm thrown across his chest. Sometime in the early morning hours, she must have rolled over, seeking comfort.

He liked the way her body felt next to his and the smell of the shampoo she'd used in her hair. He could get used to waking up beside this woman.

It would never happen.

Sunny wasn't the woman for him. Between their two careers, they'd never see each other. She'd be on tour. He'd be deployed. Children would be out of the question. Who would take care of them? Neither one of them had the time.

He almost laughed out loud at his musings. It wasn't like Sunny Daye would have any interest in him whatsoever.

Carefully, he extricated himself from beneath her arm and stood. Once Dash was off the couch, Sunny stretched out, taking up the length of the sofa.

Dash tucked the blanket around her and turned.

A soft knock at the door captured his attention. He reached for the handle and opened it a small crack to find one of the bodyguards standing there.

"We're getting ready to roll," the guard said.

Dash nodded and whispered, "I'll inform Miss Daye. Who does the driving?"

"I will," the guard said.

Dash nodded. "I'll be sure to secure anything that might fall."

"Thanks."

Dash closed the door and turned toward Sunny. He'd rather she was buckled into a seatbelt, but he didn't have the heart to wake her when she needed the sleep. Still, she'd be better off in bed than on the couch directly behind the driver's seat.

He reached down and scooped his arms beneath her.

When he straightened, she wrapped an arm around his neck, and her eyes fluttered open. "Hey," she said.

"I thought you were asleep," he said, looking down into her clear blue eyes.

"I was, until you woke me." She looked around. "Where are we going?"

"You're going back to the bed."

She shook her head. "Can't sleep back there when the coach is moving," she said, her voice slurring slightly. "Bounces too much. I've launched into the air over a foot. It's not much fun, nor conducive to sleep."

"Then I guess you'll sleep right here on the couch." He deposited her back on the sofa.

She nodded and yawned. "I'm getting up."

"If you have another show tonight, you need rest," he said, concerned about the dark circles beneath her eyes. "Get some sleep now, while you can."

She yawned again. "I do have a show, and I will get rest. But for now, I could sure use some coffee and food." As if on cue, her stomach rumbled. "I haven't eaten since noon yesterday."

He frowned. "Why didn't you say so? You can't survive on one meal a day."

Sunny stretched. "I've survived on less."

"You relax and let me see what I can rustle up." He started to tuck the blanket around her.

She grabbed his wrist. "Really, I'm awake. I can fend for myself. You're my bodyguard, not my servant." She swung her legs over the side of the couch and sat up. "At least, let me help."

He grinned. "What? Don't you think a Delta Force operative can whip up an egg?"

"Oh, I'm sure you can, but I like my eggs the way I like my eggs."

"Not at all picky, are you?" He laughed. "We'd better do it quickly before they crank this baby up. It'll be hard to cook on bumpy roads."

A knock on the door interrupted Dash as he rummaged through the cabinets searching for a skillet.

Sunny started for the door.

He stopped her with a hand on her arm. "I'll get it."

She nodded and went back to the little kitchen, taking eggs out of the refrigerator and a skillet out of the cabinet below the counter.

Dash opened the door to find his team leader standing on the ground by the steps.

"I'll be right back," he called out to Sunny and joined Rucker outside, closing the door behind him.

"Good news," Rucker said.

"You found the man in charge of the human trafficking?" Dash asked.

"No," Rucker said, "but the team is going to escort the USO tour to its next stop."

Dash grinned, relief washing over him. "Glad to hear it. I wasn't convinced the USO's security was strong enough to keep them safe."

A knowing smile spread across Rucker's face. "In particular, to keep Miss Daye safe?"

Dash nodded. "Especially."

"How did it go last night with the pretty singer?" Rucker asked.

Dash was glad of the shadows that hid the heat creeping across his face. "All right."

"I hear you paid a visit to the refugee camp."

"We did."

"I also hear Miss Daye sang for the women and children."

"She sang a lullaby to a little girl who was distraught." Dash smiled. "It was amazing. No band, no flashy lights or stage. Just her voice."

"I've heard some of her acapella work." Rucker shook his head. "She doesn't need a band. Her voice, alone, is remarkable."

Dash couldn't agree more with his team lead.

"The guys are collecting available transport from the motor pool. They've commandeered a couple of vehicles with mounted machine guns."

"What happened to the original escorts?" Dash asked.

Rucker's lips thinned. "They're being given the day off."

"Great," Dash said. "Instead of adding to the security forces, they're replacing them with Deltas."

Rucker pounded Dash on the back. "Got that right."

"No worries." Dash sighed. "I trust our guys more than I trust anyone else."

"Thought you might," Rucker said. "I almost think it might be better to send the crew with the equipment ahead and fly Miss Daye out to her next gig instead of driving her across country."

"I thought of that, too," Dash said. "I suggested it to the tour coordinator. He said they didn't have money in their coffers to pay for the flight."

"Yet they have money to pay for a funeral?" Rucker shrugged.

"He seemed to think they had sufficient security." Dash glanced down the line of vans, trucks and motor coaches. "I'm not convinced."

"Me either," Rucker said. "I'm just glad we'll be part of the convoy. If the traitor who's negotiating the human trafficking deals decides to make another attempt to capture Miss Daye, we'll be ready."

"In the meantime," Dash nodded toward the refugee tent, "what's going to happen to the displaced women and children?"

"After intelligence has had their day with them, they'll be turned over to a local government entity and returned to their homes." Rucker's lips pursed. "Sadly, many of them don't have homes to go to. They'll end up in some permanent refugee camp until they can be placed."

At that moment, Lance, Tank and Blade arrived on a vehicle with a machine gun mounted in the middle. Lance stood behind the gun, Tank drove and Blade rode shotgun.

"Looks like you don't get to have all the fun after all," Blade called out. "We're going along for the ride."

Another vehicle, just like the first, arrived with Dawg manning the machine gun, Mac driving and Bull riding shotgun.

Bull leaped out of the vehicle and approached Dash carrying a satchel and his go bag. He handed the satchel to Dash. "You'll find additional ammo in there, in case we're attacked. We have more in the vehicles if you run out."

"Thanks," Dash held the heavy satchel in one hand and reached for his duffel bag. "Thanks. I might need extra clothes."

The men gathered around Rucker and Dash.

"It's been a while since we've been on convoy duty." Blade clapped his hands. "Should be fun."

"Yeah, right," Tank said.

Their CO arrived and stood in the middle of the group. "I'm counting on you all to keep Miss Daye safe on the remainder of the tour."

"When we get there, do we get to listen to her concert?" Lance asked.

"You can listen all right, as long as you remember you're on guard duty." The CO rested his hands on his hips. "Do I need to go with you guys to keep you in line?"

Rucker grinned. "Yes, sir! Then you can hear Miss Daye sing as well."

"I got to catch her show here," the colonel said. "If you don't think you'll need me, I'll stick around here and keep an ear to the ground with the intel folks." He handed Dash a satellite phone. "Keep in touch."

"Yes, sir," Dash said.

Rucker climbed into the lead vehicle Tank was driving.

Dash entered the motor coach to find that Sunny had finished cooking the eggs and dished the food out onto two plates she'd laid on the dining table. "Better hurry and eat," she said. "Once this buggy starts rolling, it'll get crazy bumpy. The roads aren't the greatest."

As he sat at the table, Dash fitted the two-way radio ear bud in his ear and went through the motions of performing a communications check with his team. When he finished, he glanced across the table at Sunny and grinned. "Thank you for breakfast. I owe you one."

She shook her head. "Not at all. I enjoyed cooking for you. I don't get to do it often in the States. We're always on the go."

While Sunny and Dash scarfed down their meal, the bodyguard driver slipped behind the steering wheel and cranked up the motorhome.

"Let the adventure begin," Sunny said with a grin and took her plate to the sink.

Dash swallowed his last bite and followed suit. As he reached around Sunny to lay the plate in the sink, the vehicle lurched forward.

Dash braced his hands on either side of Sunny, using his body to hold her steady until the motion of the vehicle steadied and they could get back to the couch.

"Are you going to be all right back here without a seatbelt?" he asked when they both moved away from the counter.

She rummaged in the creases of the couch and unearthed a seatbelt. "I'll be fine. Now that my stomach isn't protesting, I can get that sleep I need before I have to perform again."

"I'll be in the passenger seat. All you have to do is yell, and I can be back here in a second."

He held onto the cabinet above her head to keep from falling.

She looked up at him. "I'll be fine. Go. Let me sleep."

When he turned to leave her, she reached out and grabbed his arm.

"Dash," she said.

He liked the way her hand felt on his arm, almost as much as he'd liked the way her body had felt pressed against him in her sleep. His groin tightened. "Yes, ma'am."

"Thanks for being here for me."

He nodded, lifted her hand and pressed a kiss to

the backs of her knuckles. "My pleasure." Then he grabbed his rifle and handgun and joined the driver in the front of the vehicle. He hoped that by being in the front of the vehicle, he could ignore the fact he had a hard-on for the woman behind him.

The convoy moved out of the forward operating base and onto the road leading southwest to the next concert venue.

Used to getting in and out of areas by way of helicopter, Dash was uneasy about traveling by road. The Taliban liked using IEDs to target convoys. He worried about his friends in the lead vehicle. They would be the ones to take the first hit, which would stall the convoy and allow the Taliban to attack.

All in all, he wasn't happy about the situation. Still, he was glad his team was with him.

For the first twenty miles, the road was flat with no vegetation or buildings on either side. They could see for miles. Then they entered a hilly area where the road curved in and around hills and valleys.

Dash tensed. Along any one of the curves, the enemy could be waiting to ambush them. He glanced over his shoulder to discover that Sunny was awake, sitting up with her guitar on her lap.

After a few random strums, she settled into a song and hummed, making notes in a pad in front of her. She played the tune over and over again. It took shape with more humming and more note jotting. Slowly, she added words to the notes...a haunting melody about being lost in the dark and being found.

With his focus on the road, he allowed the music to soothe him, much like the lullaby had calmed the child in the tent.

Sunny most definitely had a gift, and she was much better off singing solo. Her partner hadn't been half as talented as she was. It took him dying for her to come into her own and for her talent to shine through.

Dash refused to let her light be snuffed out or lost to the rest of the world. She had so much to give in her life.

The hills became more rugged, the valleys narrower and tight.

When they rounded a curve or climbed to the top of a pass and looked down, Dash strained his eyes to see ahead.

In one particular canyon-like area, the caravan of vehicles came to a sudden stop.

Dash's hands tightened around the stock and barrel of his rifle. "What's going on up there?" he asked into his mic.

"Got a herd of goats clogging the road," Tank reported from the lead vehicle.

"Could be a diversion," Dash suggested.

"Keeping our eyes open," Rucker promised.

A hand touched Dash's shoulder. "What's wrong?" Sunny asked.

"Goats on the road." He glanced over his shoulder at her. "You might want to get down and stay down until we make it through these hills."

"Goats aren't going to hurt us," she said and then frowned. "Are they?"

He shook his head. "No. But if they were put there to slow us down, we might be in for a fight. Please, get down and stay down. But first, double-check the side door to make certain it's locked."

She nodded. "Okay. Will you come back with me?"

He shook his head. "Not yet. If we get into a fire-fight, I want to see it coming and help, if possible."

Her hand tightened on his shoulder. "Be careful."

"I will be. I'm more concerned about you. If bullets start flying, the walls of this coach won't be enough of a shield. That's why I ask that you stay down. We don't want you catching a bullet."

"Or you and Marcus, our driver." She gave Marcus a tight smile. At Dash's pointed glance, she raised her hands. "Okay, if it makes you feel better, I'll stay back here and hunker down."

As Sunny backed away, Dash stared ahead and to the sides, looking up at the rugged bluffs rising up on either side of the caravan.

He didn't like sitting still. The lack of movement gave terrorists the opportunity to lock in their aim and take out their opponents like a bunch of sitting ducks.

"Status of the goats?" Dash asked.

"Running down the middle of the road," Tank said. "I'm trying to ease through them, but they're kind of dumb or have a death wish. They keep crossing in front of me."

Dash's hand tightened on his rifle, an uneasy feeling creeping over him. "Do you see a shepherd?"

"Off to one side," Blade's voice cut in. "Looks like a kid."

"Armed?" Dash asked.

"With a stick," Blade responded.

"I don't like it," Dash said.

"Neither do I," Rucker said into Dash's ear. "My gut is telling me to get the hell out of here. Pronto. Pedal to the metal, Tank."

"Survival of the fittest," Tank grumbled.

Moments later, the vehicles of the caravan lurched forward one after the other.

As they passed a narrow valley on their right, a flash of light caught Dash's attention. He glanced in that direction.

"Damn," he said into his mic. "Got half a dozen bogeys on motorcycles coming around the corner. Get ready for some fireworks."

"We don't know their intent," Rucker said. "Don't fire until they do."

With the riders crowding around Sunny's motor coach, Dash didn't like that he couldn't start eliminating them one by one.

Over his shoulder, he called out. "If you're not down, now would be a good time."

"I'm on the floor. It's as close to the ground as I can get," Sunny shouted over the sound of the motorcycle engines.

"Hang on," Dash said as the riders caught up and rode alongside. "It's about to get crazy out there." He lowered his window and poked his rifle out. The driver did the same, a handgun resting in his lap as he steered the giant coach one-handed.

Dash aimed for the nearest rider. He wouldn't pull the trigger until they fired the first shot.

He didn't have to wait long before one of the cyclists raised a handgun and fired at their motorhome, piercing the front windshield in the middle.

The driver jerked backward, the motorhome swerved to the left and would have run off the road if Dash hadn't lunged across the console. He grabbed the steering wheel and righted the vehicle.

"Marcus." Dash held onto the steering wheel but couldn't control the speed. "Marcus, are you still with us?"

The bodyguard clutched his arm. "I'm hit," he said through gritted teeth."

"Can you hold on until we can get somewhere safe?"

The man nodded his head. "But I can't steer."

"I'll steer, you accelerate and brake."

"Okay," Marcus said through gritted teeth.

"What's going on?" Sunny had crawled up the center of the coach to where Dash was manhandling the steering wheel.

"Marcus's been hit."

Another shot was fired at the front windshield.

Dash ducked instinctively. The bullet went wide. He cursed and hunkered as low as he could and still see over the dash.

"Let me drive. You shoot," Sunny said.

"No. They might hit you."

"And they might hit me anyway if you don't start shooting back." She eased her way forward, sliding beneath him to grab the steering wheel. "Go! Marcus and I can handle this. You handle the shooters."

Dash didn't like that Sunny was exposed in the front seat. But he couldn't protect her if he was dead. He returned to his seat, took up his rifle and focused on killing as many of the bastards as he could, as quickly as he could.

He refused to let one more bullet hit their windshield and potentially hurt or kill Sunny. "Got problems back here," he said through his clenched jaw.

"We're on our way back," Rucker said.

"Just keep this train moving," Dash said. "We can't stop, or they'll be all over us."

"We're on our way forward to help," Mac said. "Hang tight. We're coming up on your left."

Dash glanced in the rearview mirror on his side

of the coach. The roads had very little room on either side.

"Sunny, can you steer the motorhome to the right?"

"Yes," Sunny said, and the coach swerved to the right then straightened.

Another shot hit the passenger door and came all the way through, nicking Dash's calf. He hissed.

"What?" Sunny shot a glance his way.

"Nothing," Dash said. He aimed his rifle out the window at one of the men on a motorcycle. As soon as he could get a bead on him, he pulled the trigger.

The motorcycle swerved right, the wheel turning so sharply, the rear of the vehicle flipped over the front, throwing the rider through the air.

"Got one coming up on the right," Marcus said.

Dash had one on his side within range. He aimed and fired, hitting his mark. Then he lunged from his seat, leaned between Sunny and Marcus and waited for the cyclist to come even with them. He fired two rounds, one of which hit the man, sending him tumbling over the side of the road and down into a gully.

Four more men on motorcycles raced toward them.

CHAPTER 6

SUNNY HELD on tightly to the steering wheel of the motor coach. It was larger than anything she'd ever driven and harder to turn.

The trucks and vans in front of her continued to move forward, picking up speed.

The goats scattered to each side of the road.

One of the motorcyclists ran into one, flipped his cycle and flew through the air.

Good, Sunny thought. She hoped he was incapacitated from his fall. That was one less man for them to deal with.

But there were so many more.

At the rate they were moving in on them, Dash wouldn't be able to keep up.

He dropped back into his seat, reloaded his rifle with a fresh magazine and glanced in his side mirror.

Her back aching from leaning over Marcus to

steer the coach, Sunny couldn't give up. She glanced in the side mirror and almost cried with relief.

Like avenging angels, Dash's team converged on their motorhome from the rear. Dawg, on the gun turret, let loose a round from his machine gun. Taking out two more of the men on bikes.

Directing her focus forward, Sunny smiled. In front of them, Rucker's transport with Lance manning his machine gun, raced toward them, firing at the attackers with deadly bursts of bullets.

Through all the gunfire, the caravan continued forward, pushing through the hills until they emerged onto a flat, clear area close to a small village.

The remaining men on motorcycles peeled away from the caravan and disappeared back into the hills.

"Roger," Dash said. He turned to her. "We're going to stop and assess the damage."

"Thank God," Sunny said. "Marcus needs his wound looked at, and so do you."

"I'm fine," Dash said.

Marcus eased up on the accelerator, and the coach slowed until it came to a stop behind the van in front of them.

Sunny let go of the steering wheel, pressed a hand to the small of her back and straightened. She'd never been so glad to stop on a road trip.

Dash brushed her hand to the side and rubbed the small of her back where it ached from standing in an awkward position, steering the motorhome.

He leaned close to her ear, his chest touching her back, making her warm. "Sunny, I need you to stay inside the vehicle."

"But we need to get Marcus out of his seat and down on the ground to have a medic look at him," she said.

"I can get out on my own," Marcus said. "My legs are fine, it's my arm that's injured."

"Yeah, and you've lost a significant amount of blood," she said.

"I'll be fine," he insisted.

"We'll help him down," Dash promised. "I can't have you standing around outside. Someone might see that as an opportunity to swoop in and steal you away."

She shivered. "I don't want that to happen."

"Then close and lock the doors behind us, and stay put."

She nodded. "I will."

Dash left the motorhome through the passenger door, walking around the front of the vehicle to the driver's side.

Sunny reached across and pressed the lock on the passenger door.

Dash opened the driver's door and held out his hand to Marcus.

"I can do this on my own," Marcus insisted.

"Humor me," Dash said. "Take my hand and lean on me if you need to."

Marcus held onto the doorframe, placed his hand in Dash's and let the soldier guide him to the ground.

Sunny winced when Marcus winced, only imagining the pain the bodyguard was feeling.

When Marcus's feet hit the ground, his knees buckled. He would have fallen if Dash hadn't been there to hold him up.

Easing him out of the way, Dash closed the driver's door and nodded to Sunny. "Lock it."

She did and stared through the window, feeling useless and the root of their problems. If she was the one they really wanted, everyone in the caravan was at risk because of her. Marcus had just taken a bullet because of her.

She glanced toward Dash's leg and noticed a long, dark stain on his trousers. He'd been hit worse than he'd let on and was still bleeding.

Sunny unlocked the door, pushed it open and stepped one foot out on the stairs. "Dash, you're bleeding."

"I know I am. It's not much, just a flesh wound." His brow furrowed. "I'd feel a whole lot better if you got back into the vehicle and locked the door. I have my hands full here. I don't want to drop Marcus to defend you."

"Sorry." Sunny backed up the step, climbed into the driver's seat, closed the door and locked it with a loud click.

Dash helped Marcus sit on the steps, and then called out, "Bull, got a patient for you."

The man Dash had introduced as Bull dropped down from his vehicle and hurried over. He pulled a packet out of his bulletproof vest and spread it out on Marcus's knees. It contained gauze , a tube of glue and medical tape. He cut the sleeve of Marcus's shirt away and inspected the wound.

Bull flushed it with a water bottle, dried it with gauze and glued the edges together. For a full two minutes, he pinched the skin together until the glue dried. With the wound closed, he packed it with gauze and wrapped the arm. And he did all that in less than five minutes.

Sunny watched in amazement as the medic worked his magic with the bodyguard. When he was finished, he started to pack up his kit.

Sunny lowered the window. "Be sure to look at Dash's leg wound," she said softly.

"You got hit?" Bull asked.

Dash glared up at Sunny, and then turned back to Bull. "Just a nick. I can take care of it myself."

"Let's see," Bull insisted.

Dash turned to show his teammate the leg with the blood on his trousers.

"Either drop your drawers or let me cut them away," Bull demanded.

"It can wait until make the next FOB," Dash said.

Bull shook his head. "The longer you wait to close it, the more infected it will get."

"I'll take my chances." Dash glanced toward the hills behind them. "We need to get moving before that gang of goons decides to regroup and come back for more."

"You need to take care of your leg," Sunny said.

His lips firmed. "I'm fine. Let it go."

Sunny started to argue, but she could see the tension in Dash's jaw. He was worried about another attack. "Fine. Let's get going."

One of her bodyguards helped Marcus into one of the other vehicles, and the other two guards headed for Sunny's motorhome.

She hurried to unlock the driver's door and scooted back as the one called David checked the engine, making sure it hadn't taken a bullet to a critical area. When he was sure it was okay, he took the driver's seat.

The other bodyguard, Ray, glanced at Dash as they stood beside the coach.

Dash lifted his chin in the direction of the front passenger seat. "You can ride shotgun. Just be ready in case those guys show up again."

The man nodded and slid into the seat beside the driver.

Sunny rushed to the door leading into the living area and unlocked it.

Dash stood at the bottom of the steps, looking up into her face. "Still want me to ride in your unit?"

She reached out her hand. "Of course, I do. Why wouldn't I?"

"I'm not sure I was much help."

"Don't be ridiculous," she said. "Of course, you were. You got several of them even before your team arrived with the machine guns."

"We should have been better prepared for a flank attack."

"You couldn't know they would be there. Even your guys in the lead didn't know they would attack. They seemed to come out of nowhere."

"But they didn't. The conditions were right for an ambush, and we didn't take enough precautions."

"You did what you could. And you took over for Marcus when he couldn't manage the steering wheel. That in itself could have been a complete disaster. If we'd crashed, those people would have been on us so fast, your guys wouldn't have gotten there in time to keep them from taking what they wanted."

"You took over steering from me," he said. "You kept us going."

"It was a team effort." She held out her hand. "Come inside. Like you said, we need to get moving again."

His teammates climbed into their respective vehicles and went in opposite directions to get to the front and rear of the convoy.

Dash took Sunny's hand, walked up into the camper and pulled her into his arms. He crushed her to his chest for a long time. So long, that the driver shifted into gear and fell in behind the van in front of them. They continued their journey to the next forward operating base and a crowd of military personnel who were eager to see Sunny Daye's performance.

Dash backed into a wall to steady himself and her as the motorhome rumbled down the uneven road, bouncing and swaying.

Sunny liked how solid the man was. She felt safer with him than she'd felt at any other time in her life. "I wish I could stay like this forever."

He brushed the hair out of her face and kissed her forehead. "We should take a seat before we're thrown across the room."

She sighed and nodded. Then she took his hand and led him to the couch.

Dash sat first and pulled her down into his lap. When he winced, Sunny leaped to her feet at the same time as they hit a dip in the road that sent her flying back into his arms.

"Oh, Dash, I'm sorry." She pushed against his chest and stared into his face. "You have to be hurting, and here I am sitting on you."

He laughed and pulled her closer. "I don't feel the pain. But I feel something far better."

Her cheeks heated. She could feel the evidence of

his desire pressing against where her bottom met his lap. "As tempting as that sounds, I'd feel terrible if you bled out on me because I was too selfish to check your injury."

"I told you. I'm fine. It's just a flesh wound." He tried to pull her back into his arms.

Sunny pushed away and stood, holding onto the wall beside her. "If it's really just a flesh wound, why is it still bleeding?" Sunny gave Dash a narrow-eyed glance.

"Think of it as pushing all the impurities out of my body."

Sunny snorted, reached into a drawer and pulled out a pair of scissors. "Now, you can either drop your pants or let me cut away the fabric so I can see what we have…"

"I knew you couldn't resist seeing me naked." Dash winked and reached for the button on his camouflage trousers.

Sunny wanted to tell him she wasn't that interested in his naked body as much as she wanted to make sure he wasn't grievously injured. But that would be the truth and a lie. She wanted both. The thought of seeing his magnificent body without a thread of clothing made her weak in the knees.

"Just drop your drawers unless you want me to cut away your trousers with you in them." Sunny held up the scissors with a maniacal look in her eyes.

"I kind of need my pants," Dash said. "I don't have

a spare anywhere near this convoy."

"Then I suggest you drop them."

Dash glanced toward the guys up front.

"If you want some privacy, we can take you back to the bedroom," she said.

"That would be better," he said.

"I would think you couldn't be shy around other men. Not in the Army. Don't you all shower in the same shower tent or barracks?"

"We do," he admitted. "But we don't normally have a woman in the mix. That changes the whole dynamic."

"You're stalling and those pants aren't down." She leaned toward him with the scissors.

"Okay, okay," he said, holding up his hands. "In the bedroom."

"Go on back. I'll bring the first aid kit," Sunny said.

As Dash hurried into her bedroom, Sunny reached under a cabinet for the first aid kit. With the emergency medical supplies in hand and anticipation filling her body, she made her way carefully to the back bedroom.

Dash wasn't in the bedroom. Sunny found him in the bathroom sitting on the closed toilet, his trousers down below his knees.

Anyone else would have looked silly. But Dash was anything but silly. Thick thighs peeked out from beneath his uniform jacket.

Sunny's core tightened.

"Do you have a wash rag you don't mind getting all bloody?" he asked.

His request spurred her into action. She found a clean washcloth in a cabinet, wet it in the sink and applied it to the bullet wound. Dabbing gently. "You really need to shower and let the water wash over that hole. It would be better than a rag, pushing the germs deeper into the injured area."

"Seriously, it'll be all right until we can get to the next stop. I can shower then and seek medical attention if I need it…*after* your concert." He winked.

"*Before* my concert," she narrowed her eyes, "or I'll refuse to sing until you get it taken care of."

"You have a mean streak, don't you?" he groused.

She laughed. "Only when it counts. I'd hate for our country to lose a perfectly good Delta Force operative because he was too stubborn to seek help when he needed it."

"Fine. If we get to the FOB in time, I'll shower and seek medical attention for my booboo." He cocked an eyebrow. "Satisfied?"

"Not quite. For now, I need to apply a dressing to your booboo and wrap it up." After she'd washed it as best she could, she applied a folded gauze pad to the area and taped it in place with white medical tape. When she was done, she wrapped it with a bandage to hold everything in place.

"You're pretty good at that. Are you sure you

weren't a nurse in a former life?" Dash asked as he drew his trousers up over his boxers.

She shook her head, memories of her childhood rushing back to haunt her. "No." Sunny turned away before he could see the tears well in her eyes.

Dash caught her arm and turned her around. "Hey. Was it something I said?"

Sunny brushed away a tear. "No. Sometimes, I just get emotional."

He frowned, drew her close and tipped her chin up so that she was forced to expose the tears. "Seriously, what's wrong?"

"Besides being chased by a crazy man bent on trying to sell me to the highest bidder, being shot at by men on motorcycles and being held by a man who's breaking all my carefully constructed rules...I don't know. You tell me."

An errant tear slipped from the corner of her eye and trailed down her cheek.

"You were fine until I said something about being a nurse in a former life." Dash brushed his thumb across her cheek, wiping away the tear. "It had to be a former life if you started your singing career when you were only thirteen."

Sunny looked over his shoulder. Anywhere but into his eyes. "I never was a nurse. But I did dress wounds."

"I don't understand," Dash said.

"I was raised by my grandparents. My folks

weren't capable of taking care of a little girl. They were too strung out on drugs to give a damn about me."

"I'm sorry to hear that," Dash said. "It must have been hard for you."

Sunny shrugged. "I didn't know anything different. I was only three when I moved in permanently with my grandparents. They were my world, the parents my own mom and dad could never be."

"What does that have to do with being a nurse? Was your grandmother a nurse?"

"No. My grandfather was diabetic. If he scraped or cut himself, the wounds never seemed to heal, or healed so slowly I had to dress them daily to have any hope of them healing. The alternative was worse. He could get gangrene and have the limb amputated."

"So, you became very good at dressing wounds by doing it daily for your grandfather." Again, he brushed the hair back from her forehead. "You have a good heart, Sunny Daye."

Sunny swallowed hard and fought back the tears. "I loved my grandfather so much. He was a kind and gentle soul. His love of music inspired me to sing. He and my grandmother were with me at every concert up, until I turned twenty. By then, my grandfather's health got too bad for him to travel. I was twenty-two when he passed away. My grandmother was so sad, her health declined. She passed a year later."

"I'm sorry." He drew her into his arms and held

her for a long time.

She leaned into him. It was nice to have someone hold her when she was sad. Ray had never been good at dealing with her emotions. She'd had to suck it up and keep moving forward. Why had she stayed with him for so long?

Sunny leaned into Dash, pressing her cheek to his bulletproof vest, wishing she could feel his skin against hers.

A bump in the road sent them flying.

Dash caught her around the waist and sat on the bed, pulling her down with him. She landed in his lap.

When she started to move away, his arms wrapped around her. "You don't have to move if you don't want to," he whispered against her ear and then pressed his lips to the sensitive skin below her lobe.

Her breath caught in her throat. "I might disturb your wound," she said, leaning her head back to give him better access to her neck.

"I'm feeling no pain," he assured her, his mouth moving down the length of her neck in a slow, steady flow of kisses.

She wanted him to keep going, to capture one of her breasts between his lips, but there were two men up front, driving. They were probably wondering what was taking them so long in the back. They might even come to their own conclusions. Conclusions Sunny wished were true.

Another bump sent them flying into the air. They knocked heads as they came down on the mattress.

Dash laughed, rubbing his head. "I don't know what you find disconcerting about riding back here."

She rubbed a hand over her head where she'd hit his. "It's not safe, for one. And it's not conducive to sleeping."

"You have a point. But if you were a kid, this would be where it's at." He winked and pushed to his feet.

She chuckled. "You're right. A child would find it as much fun as a carnival ride."

Holding onto the wall, Dash reached for her hand, drawing her up into his arms. "I would have liked to continue our...conversation...but I don't want to give you a concussion. Your fans are expecting you to deliver a concert tonight."

Sunny wrapped her arms around his waist. "You're not much of a rule follower, are you?"

"I find it doesn't get you anywhere. If you want something, and you're not going to hurt anyone in the process of getting it, you should go for it."

"My grandfather felt the same way. People criticized my grandparents for encouraging me to go into the entertainment industry so young. But he always told me that, if I wanted something, I should go for it. I shouldn't let anyone get in my way or tell me I was doing it wrong." She looked up into his eyes.

"And what do you want now?" Dash asked.

She hesitated, drew in a deep breath and let it out slowly. "I want you."

His eyes flared, and his arms tightened around her. "I feel there's a *but* in there somewhere."

She nodded. "But, there are all these rules you have to follow. You're not supposed to fraternize in a war zone. I had a few of my own rules where my bodyguards are concerned. We can't just ignore everything." Her heart skipped several beats at the hunger in Dash's eyes. "Can we?" she whispered.

"To hell with the rules," Dash said and crushed her to him, claiming her lips.

They didn't come up for air until the coach hit another bump in the road.

"You're going to end up hurt if we don't move forward in this tank," Dash said. "Come on. We can continue this discussion when we make our next stop."

He led her out of the bedroom and into the living area. The two men up front were deep in a conversation about sports. They weren't aware of what had happened between Dash and Sunny.

At least, Sunny hoped they weren't. She didn't want to get Dash in trouble for kissing her. She wondered just how much trouble he could get into for kissing her...?

If it wasn't much, she'd like him to do it again.

To hell with the rules.

CHAPTER 7

DASH SETTLED Sunny on the couch, fetched a pillow for her and insisted on fastening her seatbelt. She laid her head on the pillow and closed her eyes. To avoid further temptation, Dash sat across from her, watching her chest rise and fall as she slept. She was a beauty, her golden hair pilling around her shoulders, her eyelashes making dark crescents on her cheeks and her very kissable lips were a natural rosy pink.

His groin tightened. God, he wanted the woman. Rather than continue to torture himself by staring at what he couldn't have, he rose from his seat and joined the men up front.

"How's it going?" he asked, leaning through the gap between the seats to stare out at the road ahead.

Paul dipped his head toward a device in the dash. "From what I can tell, by the GPS, we should arrive at our destination within the next twenty minutes."

"That close?" Dash glanced out at the flat, barren surroundings and wondered why the people who lived here fought for this dried-up land.

He supposed that if it was all you knew, and your entire family and all the generations of your family before them had lived their lives there, it was home.

Even Killeen, Texas had more vegetation to offer than the terrain they were passing through.

Soon, the buildings and tents of the forward operating base appeared ahead.

Dash glanced back at Sunny. She sat up and rubbed the sleep from her eyes. "Are we there yet?" she asked and yawned.

"Almost."

"Good. I'd like to get out and stretch my legs. I haven't worked out in a couple days, and I'm feeling it." She stretched her arms in the air, pulling her shirt tight over her breasts.

Dash swallowed a groan. He shouldn't be thinking about what he'd like to do with her beautiful body, when she was the target of someone who wanted to take her and, possibly, sell her to some lowlife pimp or a sheik with a harem full of stolen women.

He turned to the view ahead. "Hopefully, they have sufficient room inside the wire for you to take a leisurely stroll."

She yawned. "One way or another, I need a walk before I get on stage."

"You mean you don't get enough exercise during your performance?"

"It's a different kind of exercise," she said. "I come away exhausted. A walk before clears my mind and calms me before I have to be on."

"I'll see what we can manage. I don't want you too close to the outside fence in case someone tries to take a shot at whoever is moving inside the wire."

She nodded. "That's the reason I haven't walked since I landed in Afghanistan. I was warned not to. But I need the exercise and the chance to clear my mind."

"Then I'll be by your side with my bulletproof vest on. For that matter, we'll outfit you with a Kevlar helmet and a vest of your own."

Sunny smiled. "Thank you. I look forward to our walk."

The motorhome pulled to a stop behind the other vehicles in the convoy while the guards at the gate made sure the vans, trucks and motorhomes were free of enemy combatants and bombs.

As they waited, soldiers searched the vehicles one by one, top to bottom and even had a military working dog walk the line, sniffing for bombs.

As the vehicles were cleared, they were allowed to enter the gate.

By the time the soldiers and the dog made it to Sunny's coach, it was late afternoon. After the inspection, Paul drove through the gate and followed the military police who led them to a location where the other vehicles were parked.

Already, roadies were unpacking the equipment and portable stage, quickly erecting everything they'd need to put on a show for the troops.

Rucker, Lance, Tank and Blade hurried over to Sunny's coach as Dash dropped to the ground and turned to help Sunny out.

"Is there anything the team can do to help?" Rucker asked.

"Talk to the roadies," Sunny said. "We're running a little behind, so they might be able to use a few extra hands to speed up the process."

More soldiers appeared from the FOB. Together, they helped the roadies unload the trucks and vans and set up the stage.

For the first few minutes, Sunny and Dash watched. He didn't like standing by while others worked hard, but he refused to leave the singer's side.

After ten minutes had passed, and the stage build was underway, Dash whispered into Sunny's ear. "Get your walking shoes on."

She nodded and climbed into her coach.

Dash waited outside, counting the seconds until she reappeared.

Rucker hurried by him carrying his bulletproof vest and helmet.

"Hey," Dash stepped in front of him. "Mind if I borrow those?"

Rucker frowned. "Sure. Why?"

"I'm taking Sunny for a walk. I promised her I'd get her a helmet and a bulletproof vest."

"Perfect. It'll save me ditching them in our vehicle." He handed the items over to Dash. "Do you need some of us to come along to escort Miss Day?"

Dash's brow furrowed. "I'll be with her every step of the way. I think we'll be okay inside the wire."

"She was inside the wire of the last FOB when she was kidnapped. What makes you think there won't be another attempt here?"

"I'll be on the alert. There's still plenty of daylight, and I'll see them coming," Dash argued. "If you recall, she was kidnapped at night while out by herself."

"True." Rucker glanced toward the three bodyguards standing by the vehicle. "Are you taking them?"

Dash frowned. "I hadn't planned on it."

"They're being paid to provide her protection."

"I'll protect her," Dash insisted.

"Miss Daye will have to relieve them of their duties. It isn't your call," Rucker pointed out.

Dash sighed. "You're right. That being true, I'm certain I don't want them and our whole team following behind us."

Rucker's brow twisted. "You like her, don't you?"

He sure as hell did. Dash shrugged as casually as he could. "What's not to like?"

"You know she's a celebrity, and you're in the Army."

"No," Dash's lips pressed together. "I didn't know that."

"I'm just saying, she might be a little out of our league."

Dash frowned. "Our league? You're not interested in her too, are you?"

Rucker chuckled. "No. I have a girl. Nora's everything I could ever want. I was speaking hypothetically. Why would a celebrity like Sunny Daye settle for someone like you or me? She could have her pick of men."

Dash huffed out a breath. "You think I haven't told myself that at least a hundred times?" He glanced toward the motor coach. "She's amazing. And I'm... well...I'm me."

"An impressive Delta who has saved all of our asses on multiple occasions, who fights for his country and cares what happens to women and children."

"And I'm in a completely different world than Sunny. Even if she found me interesting enough to spend time with me after all this, I'm sure she has her concert schedule, and we have our insane lives, where we can be called up at a moment's notice."

"Yeah," Rucker said. "A relationship with Miss Daye would be difficult to say the least."

"Impossible," Dash murmured, feeling a little disheartened.

"But then, I've never known anything that slowed you down when you wanted something."

"The difference here is that she's not something. She's *someone*. There's a whole different dynamic involved."

"Right. You might like her and think she's worth the effort, but she has to like you, too." Rucker pounded Dash on the back. "Good luck, man. You're going to need it if you're going after her." He tipped his chin toward the motorhome. "Speaking of the devil…"

Dash turned to see his angel standing in the door, smiling down on him.

His heart turned backflips, and his breath lodged in his lungs. Even with her hair up in a messy bun and her face free of makeup, she was beautiful and worth any amount of effort he had to employ to get her to spend time with him. It probably wouldn't lead to anything, and she'd surely break his heart, but he was willing to take the risk.

Sunny walked down the steps wearing shorts, a Dallas Cowboys' jersey and running shoes. She was so darned cute, Dash wasn't sure they'd get around the camp without a couple dozen soldiers falling in love with her along the way.

He started toward her, his hands and arms

weighted by the bulletproof vest and helmet. A glance down at the items brought a smile to his face.

Dash looked up and grinned at Sunny. "You might want to reposition your hair."

She reached up to touch her messy bun. "Really? Why?"

"You're wearing these," he said.

Her eyes widened. "You weren't kidding, were you?"

"Sweetheart, I rarely kid when it comes to beautiful women. And you, my dear, are a beautiful woman." He gave a brief chin lift. "Drop the bun to the back of your neck."

She pulled the elastic band from her hair and let the tresses fall down around her shoulders.

Thankfully, Dash's hands were too full to allow him to reach out and run his fingers through the soft, golden strands.

Twisting her hair behind her head, she applied the elastic band and secured a new messy bun at the nape of her neck.

Dash handed her the bulletproof vest. "Slide into that."

She took the vest, her arms dipping as she did. "It's heavier than you made it look."

"The better to protect you with," he said and waggled his eyebrows.

Once she had the vest on, he plunked the helmet

on her head. It fit so loosely, it came down around her ears and blocked her vision.

"Is this how it's supposed to fit?" she asked, pushing it up in the front so she could see.

Dash laughed. "No. The liner is adjustable." He took the helmet, adjusted the liner and set it back on her head.

"Better?" he asked.

She nodded. "Much." Looking up at him from beneath the rim of her helmet, her blue eyes shone. "How do I look?"

He shook his head. "Even in a helmet and vest, you're too darned cute for your own good." He glanced down at her shorts. "Do you have a burqa or something you can cover up with?"

Her brow wrinkled. "Seriously? I've seen some of the Army females out running in their shorts and T-shirts. What I'm wearing is no different."

"Sweetheart, it's a lot different." He chucked a finger beneath her chin. "I'm not sure how many people will want to tackle you for that Dallas Cowboys jersey."

"If they want it that bad, I'd gladly give it to them." She reached for the hem of her shirt and started to drag it up her torso.

Dash sucked in a breath at the first sighting of her bare midriff. "Whoa, wait a minute."

Her hands froze halfway up. "If you think the shirt will cause a riot, I'll give it away, right now."

He shook his head. "I was kidding. But if you really want to start a riot, take off that jersey and you'll have every man and some of the women on this base in a stampede to get to you." He laughed. "And not for the damned jersey. So...keep your shirt on."

She grinned and let the hem fall down around her hips. "If we're done talking, I'd like to get that walk in before I have to dress for the performance."

"I'm done." He nodded his head toward her bodyguards, who'd moved closer when she'd stepped out of her motorhome. "Are we taking all three?"

Her lips twisted as she stared at the three men. "I'd rather not, but Lloyd would insist. He's paying for them to provide my security."

"You have me for that now," Dash reminded her.

"I do." She glanced up at the clear blue sky. "And it's a beautiful day. Surely, I don't need all four of you."

He shrugged, pretending nonchalance. "Your call."

"This helmet and vest should help." She gave a quick nod. "I'm going to give them an hour off." Sunny turned to her three guards. "How's Marcus?"

"Some of the medics carried him over to the field hospital," Paul said. "He was in good spirits, just disappointed he won't be continuing on the tour."

"After being shot, you'd think he'd be glad to get a ride home."

"No, ma'am." Paul said. "He likes working with you."

Sunny smiled. "I'm glad he'll be okay." She made eye-contact with each of the remaining bodyguards. "You three can stand down for the next hour."

"But ma'am," Paul said, "at least two of us are supposed to be with you at all times."

"I have Dash and this vest and helmet. I'll be okay for an hour in the daylight."

"Ma'am," Paul shook his head. "We work for Mr. Pendleton. He's the only one who can tell us to stand down."

Sunny sighed. "Once again, rules." She shot a quick grin at Dash. "Fine. I'll speak with Mr. Pendleton. If I can find him. In the meantime, only two of you. The other can take a break. We'll need all of you during the show."

"Yes, ma'am." Paul spoke with one of other two guards. That man turned and headed for the trailer the bodyguards took turns sleeping in.

"Let's find Lloyd." Sunny glanced at Dash. "I'm sure he's in a flap that we're late getting here."

"He should be glad we got here at all."

"True." Her face sobered. "That attack shook me. I thought whoever was after me would go for another sneak attack, not a full-on, bring in the big guns kind of attack."

"Convoys are somewhat easy targets, with

everyone spread out in a long line. It made sense to make an attempt while you were on the road."

"I guess we should also be glad they used a goat herd to slow us down."

"Right. An improvised explosive device would've been a lot more deadly." Dash cupped her elbow and squeezed gently. "I'm glad you weren't hurt."

"I'm just sorry you and Marcus got hit."

"We'll live."

"I certainly hope so," she said. "What if we're not as lucky the next time?" She looked up at him with those incredibly blue eyes that made the hard core inside him melt. "I would hate it if one of your team, or any of our tour staff, were killed because someone wanted to get to me."

"My team is aware of the risks."

"Ma'am," Paul said from behind her, "we're all aware of the risks we're taking just being in Afghanistan. You can't worry about everyone. We signed up for this gig."

Sunny sighed. "I know."

They approached the area where the stage was being erected. Men were working frantically to piece together the frame and the stanchions that would hold the lights and speakers. Lloyd was in the middle of it all, calling out orders.

When he finally looked around and spotted Sunny, he picked his way through the parts to join them.

"Everything all right?" he asked and glanced at the hole in Dash's trousers. "I heard you took a hit."

Dash nodded. "I did. But it was only a flesh wound. Miss Daye played nurse and did a fine job dressing it."

"Speaking of which," Sunny said, "we need to stop by the field hospital and let them look at it. I'm no expert."

"It feels fine," he insisted. "Besides, I promised you a walk."

Lloyd frowned, looking from Dash to Sunny and back to Dash. "What walk?"

"Miss Daye would like to take a constitutional around the camp." He nodded toward the helmet and vest. "We've got her covered and think she'll be safe in broad daylight."

Lloyd's frown deepened. "Do you really think that's a good idea after what's happened in the past twenty-four hours?"

Sunny's shoulder's squared. "I need to get out and get some fresh air. Being cooped up isn't good for my voice."

"Neither are bullets and bad guys," Lloyd argued.

"I'll have Dash with me, and we'll stay close to the buildings and tents."

"And you think it's safe?" Lloyd turned his frown on Dash.

"I think she'll be all right," Dash said. "A short walk will be good for her."

"I'd like to let Paul and Stewy to take an hour off and relax," Sunny said. "They're going to be busy tonight keeping an eye on the crowd while we perform."

Before she finished speaking, Lloyd was shaking his head. "I can't let you go out practically alone."

"I won't be alone," Sunny said. "I'll be with Dash. And we're not going out. Just around the camp."

"It's too risky," Lloyd said. "You have a performance in two hours. What if you're hurt in that time? Think of all the troops who'll be disappointed."

Sunny blew out a breath. "Okay, fine. I'll make it a short walk so that Stewy and Paul can take a break when we get back." Sunny jerked her head to the side, making the helmet wobble. "Come on, guys. Let's walk."

As they left the organized chaos of setting up a show, Sunny grumbled. "I should've known he'd nix my request."

"He has your best interests at heart," Dash said.

"I know. And I don't want to disappoint the troops by getting killed or nabbed prior to the show."

"Is he always so focused on the show?"

"It's his job," Sunny said. "He takes it very seriously."

"Ever just want to make a run for it?" He reached for her hand, loving the way it fit in his so perfectly.

Her fingers curled around his. "Yes…" she said, her eyes narrowing.

His pulse quickened and adrenaline shot through his veins. "On the count of three," he whispered.

"What on the count of three?" she asked in a hushed tone.

He tipped his head in the direction of the bodyguards walking behind them. He wanted her alone. There was only one way to do that. "One…"

"I don't know what you mean…"

"Run," he said under his breath. "Two…"

"Run?" she asked, turning her head right then left.

"Three." Dash gripped her hand and took off.

CHAPTER 8

SUNNY RACED to keep up with Dash. "Why are we running?"

"Because we can," he said and ducked between two tents, dragging her through with him.

"Hey!" Paul shouted.

"You heard Lloyd. We can't ditch the bodyguards," Sunny said.

"Why not?" Dash ducked low and sprinted past another tent. "Get down," he urged.

Sunny bent low. "But they're only trying to do their job."

"And they will. But we're going to make it more interesting for them." Dash lifted the flap of a tent and ducked inside, pulling her through with him. Once they were inside, he let the flap fall into place and pressed his finger to his lips. "Shh."

Footsteps crunched in the gravel outside. "Miss Daye," Paul called out.

"Miss Daye," Stewy added to the plea.

When Sunny opened her mouth to answer, Dash pulled her into his arms and claimed her lips with his.

At first, she stiffened. But as he pushed his tongue past her teeth to caress hers, she melted into his embrace, her arms going up to encircle his neck.

Yes. This was where she'd longed to be all day, confined in the motorhome with this...man.

Alone. No one else to bother them, judge them or tell them to stop.

"What the hell?" a voice said behind them.

Dash pushed Sunny behind him and spun to face the owner of the words.

A young man, who couldn't be more than nineteen, sat up on an Army cot, his body covered in a mosquito netting.

He reached for the rifle beside him, his hand closing around the stock before Dash could stop him.

"Hey, buddy," Dash whispered. "We're just waiting for someone to pass."

The soldier pulled the rifle across his lap and turning it slowly in their direction. "How about I yell and let them know you're in here?"

"Please, sir," Sunny said, scraping the helmet off her head. She dragged the elastic band out of hair and let it fall down around her shoulders in a golden cloud. "I just wanted a few minutes alone before the concert tonight."

The young man's eyes rounded. "You're… you're…"

She nodded with a smile. "Sunny Daye. And you are?"

"Dreaming," he said, setting his weapon aside. He scrambled out of the cot, grabbed a desert tan T-shirt from where it was draped across a duffel bag and pulled it over his head. "Private George, ma'am. My name is Bodie George." He stuck out his hand, and Sunny took it in hers.

"Private George, thank you for not ratting me out. I really only want a few moments alone before I get up in front of all those people." Her smile lit the interior of the tent.

Private George grinned from ear to ear. "I can't believe I'm talking to Sunny Daye. In my tent."

Sunny almost laughed at the way the boy's voice shook in his excitement. He'd tell this story for the rest of his days.

When Sunny dropped her hand to her side, the young man stared at his.

"I'll never wash this hand again," he said, his words hushed and reverent.

"Miss Daye!" Paul's voice called out nearby.

Sunny grimaced. "My bodyguard is going to be upset with me," she whispered.

"I won't tell," Private George said. "Ma'am. Could I ask one thing of you?"

"Sure," she said.

"Could I get a picture of me and you...in my tent. My buddies will never believe me."

She chuckled softly. "You bet. And if you have something you want me to sign, I'd be glad to give you an autograph."

He raised his shirt. "Would you consider signing my chest?"

Her eyes danced with humor. "I would, but even permanent markers eventually fade."

The private glanced around frantically, searching for his phone and something for Sunny to write on. When he couldn't find anything but a permanent marker, he looked down at his T-shirt. "Do you mind signing my shirt?"

She shook her head. "I don't mind at all." Sunny turned to Dash. "Would you do the honors of the photo?"

"I'd love to."

Bodie handed his camera to Dash and stood beside Sunny. She slipped her arm around him and smiled at the camera.

Dash snapped several shots before he handed the camera back to the private. "Thank you, sir," the boy said.

"You don't have to call me, sir," Dash said.

"I know, sir," the private said with a grin. "You work for a living."

"Miss Daye!" Paul called out again from a little farther away. "We're organizing a search party."

"Shoot," Sunny said. "That's our cue that the party's over." She signed the private's shirt and gave him a big hug. "Thank you for sharing your tent with us for a few short minutes. Your parents must be so proud of you. Will I see you at the concert?"

He nodded. "I'll be there with a couple of my buddies."

"Be sure to tell them that Sunny Daye stopped by your tent to meet you." She winked at him, her smile fading. "Stay safe, and make sure you go home. I want to see you at future concerts in the States."

The private stood at attention and popped a salute. "Yes, ma'am.

"Ready?" Dash held out his hand to Sunny.

She settled her helmet on her head, nodded and fit her hand in his. "Let's go face the music."

"You meant that as a pun, right?" Dash asked as he held the tent flap open for her to pass through.

"Absolutely," she said with a grin, feeling lighter and happier than she had since she'd arrived in country.

As they walked back toward the stage, Sunny held tight to Dash's hand, liking that he was breaking the rule of no fraternization and flaunting it in front of others. He had to like her a little bit to go that far.

She also liked that he didn't treat her like a celebrity. Yeah, he protected her, but he'd do that for any woman he cared about.

Did he care about her?

His hand gently squeezed hers as if he could hear her question.

Her heart warmed and she leaned against his shoulder.

They might be worlds apart as far as their careers were concerned, but he was a man, she was a woman, and there was something brewing between them.

At least, she hoped there was.

As they rounded the end of a row of buildings, Sunny spotted Paul and Stewy ahead of them.

"If we hurry, we can catch up to them before they reach Lloyd and the stage crew." Sunny picked up the pace.

Dash matched her speed.

"Paul," she called out before he reached the end of the row of buildings.

He turned and waited for her to catch up. "Where did you go?"

"We made a PR call to a soldier. It only took a minute, and it completely made his day," Sunny said brightly. "I hope I didn't worry you," she said and smiled innocently. "If you need me, I'll be in my coach, getting ready for the show. You might want to grab something to eat and drink while I'm occupied. It's going to be a long night."

With that parting comment, she breezed past him and hurried toward her motorhome, Dash beside her all the way.

She liked having him with her but knew it wouldn't be forever. Hell, they barely knew each other.

Did he like to watch football? Sunny did. Ray hadn't liked to and went off to a jazz bar whenever she wanted to watch the Dallas Cowboys play.

She glanced up at Dash. Did he prefer beer over wine? Or was he a whiskey drinker? She'd peg him for beer. Sunny liked a cool beer on a hot day. Ray had only drunk rum and coke.

Did Dash like mountains or beaches? Where would he spend his honeymoon when he finally let himself fall in love?

As she climbed up into her coach, she sighed. Why did she care? They'd never be together beyond this USO gig in Afghanistan. He had his career; she had hers. They were so diametrically opposed that she couldn't see any way it would work out, even if they tried.

Was it wrong of her to want more time with Dash?

She sighed again.

"Are you tired?" he asked as he entered the motorhome behind her.

"Not really." Hell, her blood was still zooming through her veins from the kiss in the tent. Too bad the tent had been occupied, she would've liked to extend that kiss to a little heavy petting. Her fingers burned to touch his skin, all over his body.

"You just sighed again." Dash gripped her arms and turned her to face him. "What's wrong?"

"Nothing," she said, without meeting his gaze. If she looked up at him, he might see in her face all the longing she was feeling for a man she'd only just met.

He touched a finger beneath her chin and raised her face, forcing her to look him in the eye. "You were smiling just a minute ago. Now, you look all down in the dumps."

She forced a smile to her lips. "Is that better?"

He shook his head. "No. That's not a real smile. It's actually kind of creepy." He bent to touch his lips to her forehead. "I know you don't know me from Adam, but I'm actually a good listener, if you want to talk."

And tell him that she wanted him? No way.

That would be pretty pathetic for the talent to hit on the bodyguard.

"Thank you. I'm really fine. I just need to get ready for the show tonight."

He stared down at her a moment longer, his hands still resting lightly on her arms.

Then he let his arms fall to his sides. "I wish Private George hadn't been in his tent today."

She smiled a real smile. "Me, too."

He cupped her cheek in his palm. "I wanted that kiss to go on a lot longer."

Her heart pounded against her ribs, and her breath came in ragged gasps. "Me, too."

His head lowered until his lips hovered over hers. "I can't resist."

She leaned up on her toes, closing the distance, sealing her mouth over his.

Me, too.

And therein lay the problem. She couldn't resist this Delta Force soldier.

But resist, she must. Anything she might consider with him would be short-lived and heartbreaking when they had to part ways.

A little devil in the back of her mind reminded her, *Isn't it better to have loved and lost than never to have loved at all?*

Even if it was only for a few days on the road across Afghanistan?

DASH LET Sunny take the lead on the kiss. If she wanted to end it sooner, he wouldn't stop her. But boy, he didn't want it to end. He pushed his tongue past her teeth, stroking hers in a long steady glide.

He had the intense urge to sweep her up into his arms and carry her back to the bedroom and make mad, passionate love to her.

What was keeping him from doing just that? They

were finally alone in the motor coach. If they locked the doors, no one would walk in, unless they let them in.

Dash glanced at the clock. Sunny had less than an hour to prepare for her performance. He didn't want to rush her through making love. When he made love to her, he wanted to take his time exploring every inch of her body. He wanted to take her with his mouth and play her until she came.

And that was assuming she wanted it, too. One hour wasn't enough to accomplish all that, and Sunny needed the time to apply stage makeup and choose a costume for the performance.

Setting her at arm's length, Dash sighed.

She laughed. "Now, you're sighing."

"I want so much more than what we have time for."

"Like what?" she whispered, touched her fingers to his bulletproof vest. She opened the vest and helped him slide it over his shoulders, lowering it to the floor.

"Like what you're doing," he said and cupped the back of her neck, drawing her to him for a kiss that lasted only a moment. "As much as I want to make love to you, you need to get ready."

"Or Floyd will show up at my door demanding I appear on the stage ASAP." She took one of his hands in hers and carried it up to her lips, pressing a kiss to his palm. "Do you really want to make love to me?" she asked, her voice no more than a whisper.

He laughed. "Yes. More than I want to take my next breath. You're beautiful. You have the voice of an angel. What mortal man wouldn't want to make love to you?"

She sighed again. "What if I couldn't sing? What if I was just like any other woman?"

"I'd still want to make love to you," he said. "It's what's in your heart that makes you so beautiful." He brushed his thumb across her lips. "I saw you with those refugees. You really cared about them. And with Private George—you didn't brush him off, too busy to talk to a fan. You treated him like you cared. You're kind, you're funny and you're real. How many celebrities are?

"More than you would know," she said. "We're all just people like anyone else. We want to be loved for who we are, not what we can do. One day, the beauty will fade, the fingers will grow gnarled and the vocal cords will dry up. What will be left?"

He pulled her in his arms. "A warm, caring person, who can be loved for the beauty in her heart."

She stared up into his eyes, tears filling hers.

"Now, don't cry." He pressed a kiss to each of her eyelids. "You'll get all red and puffy."

She laughed. "I can't have that. It'll disappoint the troops. I'm supposed to make them happy and forget that they're thousands of miles away from home, missing their families."

"That's right. Once again, caring enough about others to help them through some tough times." He kissed the tip of her nose. "Now, go get ready. While I'm watching out for you, I get to hear you sing. I was hoping to catch your concert. Now, I can. I hear you're amazing." He winked.

"So I'm told," she said. "I'll sing a song especially for you."

"I've only had one other woman sing a song especially for me."

"Oh?" Sunny's eyebrow rose. "The hussy."

He laughed out loud. "Don't be calling my mother a hussy. She sang to my sister and me every night when we went to bed, until we were about ten years old. I'd stay awake as long as I could, just to hear her sing."

"She must be an amazing woman," Sunny said.

"To put up with me and all my shenanigans, she was," he said.

"Was? Is she still alive?"

He shook his head. "Both my parents passed a couple of years ago, within six months of each other."

"I'm sorry."

"Dad died of a heart attack. Mom missed him so much, she died of a broken heart."

Sunny laid her hand on his arm. "And now, they're together in heaven."

He nodded. "Knowing they're together, makes it a little easier to accept that I've lost both parents."

"And you're lucky you still have your sister," Sunny reminded him.

"I am. Although there have been some scares with her." He brushed a strand of her hair back from her forehead. "It's getting late. You need to get ready."

She glanced at the clock, and her eyes widened. "Yikes!" She ran for the closet, selected clothing, and dashed to the bathroom.

"I'll be out in a minute," she called out. Then she poked her head around the door and gave him a sly grin. "You wouldn't happen to want to join me in the shower, would you?"

He scowled. "Don't tempt me, woman. It would be more than a moment, if I did."

"Thought I'd ask." And she was gone. The next thing Dash heard was the sound of water running in the little bathroom.

Yes, he'd been tempted to take her up on her offer to shower with her. Maybe he'd get one while she was doing her makeup.

Not long after, the water cut off, and Sunny emerged from the bathroom with a towel turban on her head and wearing a slick, pink silk robe.

Dash groaned.

"What?" she asked.

"Nothing a cold shower might cure." He rummaged in his duffel bag he'd left on the floor earlier and pulled out a fresh T-shirt, clean trousers and boxer briefs. "I'll only be a moment."

"Take your time. I'll be here for a minute, applying my usual stage makeup and blowing my hair dry."

Dash entered the tiny bathroom, still steamy from Sunny's shower and smelling like her shampoo.

God, he wished he'd taken her up on the shower with her. Then again, he knew the few minutes she had to get ready wouldn't be long enough.

Setting the temperature to cool, Dash removed the bandage Sunny had applied so expertly, stepped beneath the spray and washed away the dust and dirt from the mission and the day of travel. His wound stung but the water washed away the dried blood and dirt.

He didn't take too long as he knew the tanks in motorhomes didn't contain a whole lot of water. She'd need it for the next couple of days, if they didn't refill it at each stop.

Once he was done, he dried off, dressed in his underwear, camouflage trousers, a T-shirt and a fresh uniform jacket. When he stepped out of the bathroom, Sunny was blowing her hair dry, using a round brush. When she was done, she used a curling iron to put waves back into her hair. She'd applied makeup to her face and eyes.

The whole process of hair and makeup made Dash glad he wasn't a woman, and even happier that Sunny was.

When she was finished with her hair, she entered her bedroom to change into the sequined royal blue dress she'd had hanging on a hook.

Dash walked to the front of the motorhome and glanced out the window.

The road crew had completed the stage setup, and the band was working the kinks out of the speakers and their instruments. The troops were already crowding into the area in front of the stage.

A sound behind him made him turn.

Sunny stood in the royal-blue, sequined dress and a pair of glittery silver high heels. "What do you think?"

"Wow." Dash crossed to her and gathered her in his arms. "You look amazing."

Her cheeks reddened beneath the stage makeup. "Thank you," she said.

A knock on her door made her back out of Dash's arms.

Dash opened the door to Lloyd Pendleton. The USO tour director smiled up at her. "Thank goodness. You're on in ten."

She nodded. "I was just about to leave."

"Good. Good," Lloyd said. "Everything's ready. We had a lot of unexpected assistance from a building contractor in the area. He was able to get his crew in to help ours get the stage up and running in record time." He turned and headed toward the stage, talking to himself about things that still needed to be done.

Dash captured Sunny once more and kissed her forehead. "What's it they say in showbiz?"

"Break a leg?" Sunny said with a mischievous smile.

"Yeah. That's it. Only I'm afraid to say it for fear it will happen in those shoes."

She laughed. "I'll be fine. I wear these shoes a lot. I can handle it."

Nevertheless, Dash scooped her up in his arms and carried her all the way to the back of the stage, across uneven gravel.

Already, he could hear the roar of the crowd of soldiers waiting for Sunny Daye to boost their spirits and give them a great show.

"I could've gotten here without the lift," she said, her arm draped across his shoulders.

"And ruin those sparkly shoes in the gravel?" Dash shook his head. "I couldn't disappoint your fans."

She laughed and kissed his cheek. "Aren't you afraid you'll get in trouble for too many public displays of affection."

He snorted. "Anyone who hit me up with those kinds of charges would only do so because they were jealous."

"Jealous because you're with a celebrity?" she asked.

"Jealous because I'm with a kind, caring and beautiful woman, who just so happens to be a celebrity." He kissed her full on the lips before he set her on her feet near the stage. "Now, where do you want me? I don't mind standing in front of you with my bullet-proof vest, deflecting bullets, but your fans might protest." He frowned. "Actually, shouldn't you be wearing the vest and helmet you had on earlier?"

She frowned. "You think anyone will take a shot at me? Aren't we far enough away from the outer fence that it would be difficult for a sniper to pick me off?"

His chest tightened. "I hope so. Really, I could have someone run back to the motorhome and get the protective gear."

Sunny shook her head. "I'll take my chances. These guys don't want to see me sing and dance in a helmet and bulletproof vest. They want to be reminded of home where they don't have to worry as much about being shot."

"I'd feel a lot better if you wore a vest. I don't suppose you could get one on under that dress...?" He ran his gaze over the length of the short, sequined dress and shook his head. "No. That would not be possible."

Sunny chuckled. "Yup, not possible. There's only room for me under this. And it's itchy. As soon as the concert is over, it's coming off."

Dash growled low in his chest. "Mmm. I like the sound of that."

Her eyes flared, and her lids drooped. "I might need help getting out of it…"

"I'm here for you, sweetheart. All you have to do is ask."

With a grin, she leaned forward and kissed his cheek. "The troops are waiting. I'd better get up there and give them what they came for."

"Music," Dash clarified. "Just give them music."

"I'll save the rest for later." She winked and turned toward the stairs.

Lloyd stood at the top, a microphone in his hand. He wore a suit and tie, and his hair was slicked back. Not only was he the tour coordinator, he was also the master of ceremonies, there to introduce the acts. "Are you ready?"

Sunny nodded. "Let's do this."

Lloyd stepped out on the stage and keyed the microphone.

The audience grew silent as Lloyd made the introductions.

Dash moved around to the corner of the stage to get a better angle to watch Sunny and the audience at the same time.

"And now, please welcome Miss Sunny Daye," Lloyd said like a ringmaster at a circus.

The crowd of soldiers roared their approval, clapping, whistling and yelling out Sunny's name.

Sunny stepped out on the stage. The lights trained on her made her dress sparkle, but it was the light in her eyes and her beauty that shined even brighter.

The soldiers roared even louder.

When the band started playing, everyone grew silent, waiting for the magic of Sunny's voice.

And she didn't disappoint. From the first note to the last, she left the listeners mesmerized, including Dash.

He struggled to focus on the crowd and everything around the woman singing on the stage, when all he wanted to do was immerse himself in the beauty of her voice.

The bodyguards had positioned themselves on the fringes of the crowd, ready to step in should anyone get too close to Sunny.

Dash would leap across people, stage equipment and anything else in his way should Sunny's safety become compromised.

Despite the beauty of Sunny's music, Dash couldn't relax until the concert was over. The tension increased with each minute, until he was so tightly strung, he was ready for a fight to blow off some steam. Just not any fight that harmed Sunny.

For her encore song, she turned toward where he was standing and whispered into the microphone, "This one's for you."

He knew she was speaking to him. But the crowd had to feel like she was singing directly to them. She had that way of including every fan in the enchantment she created.

The lights dimmed as she took one last bow.

Dash climbed the stairs to the stage, hooked an around her waist and led her away. Lloyd met them at the stairs with a broad grin. "Wow, Miss Daye. Every time I hear you I think you're even better than the last. This time was no different." He reached for her hands and squeezed them gently. "Some of the men who helped erect the stage would like a chance to meet you in person."

"Miss Daye must be exhausted after such a stunning performance," Dash directed his words toward Lloyd then turned to Sunny. "Are you up for it?"

She gave a weak smile. "I am. It's part of what I do. And I really appreciate my fans. They're who got me where I am."

Lloyd clapped his hands. "Good. Then come with me. They're waiting behind the stage."

His arm still wrapped around Sunny's waist, Dash stuck to her like glue. Her three bodyguards flanked them as they stepped down from the stage and rounded it to the back where a dozen people stood ready to dismantle the equipment and load it up for their move to the next location in the morning.

One by one, Sunny greeted the men and women who'd helped in the erection of the stage and setting up equipment, thanking them by name.

"And this is Desmond Housman, the contractor who jumped in and helped us tremendously in meeting our deadline," Lloyd said. "Without him and his people, we might not have started the show on time."

"Nice to meet you, Mr. Housman," Sunny said, holding out her hand to the man.

The contractor was a tall, imposing figure with gray hair and gray eyes. His lips barely moved into a smile as he took her hand. "The pleasure is mine. We're just glad we could help."

"They only arrived at the base a few hours earlier than you," Lloyd said. "I feel it was fate that brought them here today."

"Thank you for helping our crew."

"It was for a good cause," Housman said. "Your music is loved worldwide. Even the Afghans have heard of you."

"That's good to know," Sunny said. "Again, thank you for helping out." When she tried to pull her hand away, the contractor held on.

"I heard you had trouble on the way out here. I hope you weren't hurt." His gaze swept over her.

Dash's eyes narrowed. "She wasn't. Now, if you'll excuse us, Miss Daye has had a trying last twenty-four hours. She needs to rest before they leave in the morning."

"Of course." Still he held onto her hand a moment longer.

Dash was tense enough. He didn't need to deal

with an overzealous fan. But if the contractor didn't release Sunny's hand in the next three seconds, he was going to put his fist into the man's face.

Three...Two...

Desmond Housman let go of Sunny's hand. "Thank you for your music, Miss Daye. I hope to see you again, soon."

She nodded.

With a hand at her back, Dash led her away from the crew that was already digging into the task of dismantling the stage and packing the sound equipment and instruments.

Several people stopped them on their way back to the motorhome, congratulating Sunny on another great concert. She smiled and thanked every one of them.

By the time they reached the motorhome, Dash could feel Sunny slowing down. "Are you all right?" he asked as he unlocked and opened the door for her.

"I am. I get this way after every concert. While on stage for a couple of hours, with my game face on, I'm upbeat, outgoing and totally engaged with the audience." She laughed softly. "I think it sucks all the life out of me for the next twenty hours."

"I'll make you a cup of tea while you shower. Then you can crash and sleep until it's time to do it all again. I'll even move you to the front of the motorhome before they roll off the base tomorrow morning."

She cupped his cheek with her hand. "You're my security, not my maid. I can make a cup of tea for myself."

"You're tired. I'm wound up. Making tea will help me to relax. Now, go. Get your shower and get out of that itchy dress which, by the way, looked amazing on you." He kissed the tip of her nose. Then his lips found hers in a gentle kiss. He wanted more, but he didn't want to draw on more of her energy reserves. And he certainly wasn't going to bring up her teasing promise of more later. Not when she was so tired she could barely stand on her own two feet.

Sunny entered the motor coach and headed down the hall to the bathroom.

Dash closed and locked the door, throwing the bolt to keep any of the crew who might have a spare key from entering without permission. He didn't want anyone to disturb Sunny's rest.

Unless she wanted to be disturbed. In which case, he would gladly volunteer to be the disturber.

Wishful thinking on his part, entirely.

CHAPTER 9

TIRED TO THE BONE, Sunny stood in the bathroom, staring at her face in the mirror. The makeup hid the dark circles beneath her eyes, but it didn't hide the fact she was exhausted by more than just a stressful last twenty-four hours.

She was ready to take a break from touring. Since she was thirteen, she'd been working non-stop until the death of her partner. At the ripe old age of twenty-seven, most of her peers were on their first marriage with maybe two children.

Sunny had always wanted children and had hoped she and Ray would one day marry and have a couple of them. Now that Ray was out of her life, she could look back with a clearer understanding of her feelings for the man. He'd been with her since she was eighteen. She'd been more in love with the idea of getting married and having children than she'd been in love with the man himself.

At that moment, she couldn't even bring up an image of Ray in her mind. The only image that came to her readily was that of the rugged Delta Force soldier in the other room.

The exhaustion of moments ago faded away to be replaced by an adrenaline rush that made her blood hum and her body sing in anticipation. She'd teased him earlier about wanting more when the concert was over.

Well, the concert was over.

Sunny grabbed makeup remover sheets and scrubbed the junk off her face. Then she switched on the water and climbed beneath the spray, washing away the rest of the makeup and the hairspray that had kept her hair bouncy throughout the performance.

When she turned off the water, all that was left was Sunny. And she was on fire with a need so strong she shook with the force of it.

She stepped out of the shower, dried her body from head to toe and rubbed as much moisture out of her hair as she could. Then she brushed the tangles out, French-braided the damp tresses and slipped into a frothy, white nightgown that barely covered the white lace thong panties she put on next. If this didn't say she was ready to take their relationship to the next level, she didn't know what would.

Glancing into the mirror, she wondered if she should apply just a little makeup to brighten her cheeks and lips. She shook her head and reached for the doorknob. What she liked about Dash was that he saw her. Not just the celebrity in the sequins and heavy makeup.

Taking a deep breath and praying she hadn't read the Delta wrong, she stepped out of the bathroom and almost ran into the man she'd been thinking about.

He held up two cups of steaming brew. "Whoa, babe. This stuff is hot."

Then his brow dipped, and he let out a long low whistle. "But clearly not as hot as you."

Her cheeks heated as she lifted her chin, knowing the tips of her nipples were hardening, making dark points jut out behind the sheer fabric of her nightgown.

"Is that for me?" she asked, nodding toward one of the cups.

He swallowed hard. "Yes. Yes of course." Still, he stood without moving.

"The tea?" she prompted, fighting the urge to laugh delightedly. Her gown had the desired impact. Now all she had to do was capitalize on that impact. She wanted this man. Wanted to make love to him and feel his hard, naked body against hers.

She took the mug of tea from his hand, took a tentative sip, and then set it on the counter behind her in the bathroom. "Are you going to drink that?" Sunny nodded toward the second cup of tea.

Dash looked toward the cup as if it took great effort to drag his gaze from her. "Drink? Oh yeah. No. I think I'm done with tea." He reached around her and set the cup on the counter with hers. Then he bent to scoop her up into his arms and carried her into the bedroom. "Tell me this isn't what you had in mind, and I'll leave you alone and go take a very cold shower.

She laughed and wrapped her arms around his neck. "You told me not to wear anything so sexy unless I meant it." She stared up at him, her smile fading and her voice dropping to a husky whisper. "I mean it."

"I thought you were tired," he said, laying her on the mattress, her legs draped over the side. He leaned over her and pressed a kiss to her forehead. "You need your rest."

She reached up, wrapped her arms around his neck and pulled him down to her. "I need you."

He dragged his finger along the curve of her cheek. "I don't want to be the reason you pass out on the stage."

"Then don't stall a moment longer," she coaxed. A frown settled on her pretty brow. "Unless I've read you wrong, and you're not that into me."

"Oh, sweetheart, I'm into you in a big way," he

said. "But I don't want you to fall asleep the first time I make love to you."

She cocked an eyebrow. "Are you that mediocre that I'd fall asleep?"

"Not by a long shot, but you, on the other hand, have had a helluva night and day. You have to be ready to drop."

"I was, until I stepped into the shower...*naked*. All the water swishing over my *naked* body revived me." She looked at him from beneath her eyelashes. "What part of *naked* is not doing it for you?"

He laughed and kissed her hard on the mouth, his tongue pushing past her teeth to sweep along hers in a long, slow caress.

When he came up for air. He slipped his hands beneath the hem of her nightgown and followed the curve of her hip, dipped in at her waist and brought them to rest on the swells of her breasts.

She inhaled deeply, pressing into his palms. "I thought you'd never get there. And yet, here you are."

He leaned down and blew a stream of warm air over her turgid peaks. She could feel it through the delicate silk. "They were too tempting."

"Good," she said. "I was beginning to think I needed to get a refund on the gown, or up my game of seduction."

"Oh, babe," he growled, "your game is on, and you're winning."

"If I'm winning, why aren't you in the bed with

me?" she asked, her eyebrows raised. She patted the mattress beside her. "And you're overdressed."

"Demanding much?" he quipped and straightened.

"Damn right. I'm only in this country for a few more days. I want to spend all of them with you."

"You've got me for the duration. Only thing is that I don't pack protection when I go to the field."

A grin spread across her face. "Not to worry. This motorhome is equipped with everything from twenty-four rolls of toilet paper to all the protection you could possibly need for a year in country." She rolled to her side, reached into the nightstand drawer and pulled out a box containing two dozen condoms. "Will this be enough?"

He laughed and took the box from her, extracting one of the packets. "More than enough for the short time we'll be together." His brow furrowed again. "Are you sure this is what you want?"

She nodded. "Very much so. I've been around you now for a full twenty-four hours. It feels like it's been weeks. It's like I've known you so much longer. But if you're uncomfortable doing this, you're not obligated. I can't get you fired."

He smiled. "I've wanted this from the moment I found you."

"In the body bag?" She shook her head. "How long have you been in this country? Obviously too long, if you're wanting to make love with a corpse."

While she'd been in the shower, he'd stripped out

of the bulletproof vest and his uniform jacket. "That's just it, I didn't find a corpse in that bag. I found a beautiful, lively woman who captured me with her smile." He tugged his T-shirt out of the waistband of his trousers, pulled it over his head and tossed it to the side.

Sunny feasted her gaze on his broad shoulders and rock-solid chest. The man was beautiful, and she couldn't wait any longer to touch him, taste him and feel him moving inside her.

She sat up and loosened the belt around his waist. Then she unbuttoned his trousers, exposing the boxer briefs beneath. "Not commando?"

He shook his head. "No way. You never know when you're going to sustain an injury. Having a gorgeous nurse patch you up is one thing. Most often it's a male medic." He shook his head. "Nope. Not going there."

"Good reasoning. My grandmother always told me to wear clean underwear when I went out in case I got into a car wreck."

"Same thing," Dash said and kicked off his boots.

Sunny grabbed both sides of his trousers and tugged downward.

He took over and pushed the pants to the floor, stepping free.

Already Sunny could see the affect she had on him. His erection pushed against the fabric of his black briefs.

Her eyes widened. He was big.

"You can change your mind at any time," he assured her. "I don't want to hurt you."

"I'm not changing my mind." She reached out a hand. "I want you. Now."

He shook his head. "Not yet."

"What do you mean?" she asked.

"You're not ready."

"I've been ready since you first kissed me," she argued.

"I want to make you come before I do." He gripped the hem of her gown, tugged it up over her head then dropped it on the nightstand.

Sunny shivered as the cool night air brushed across her nipples.

For a long moment, he drank her in, making her feel more beautiful than she'd ever felt in her life.

Dash hooked his thumbs in the elastic waistband of her lacy panties and dragged them slowly over her hips and down her legs until they dropped to the floor.

Naked and aching with longing, Sunny reached out to remove the boxer briefs Dash wore.

He brushed her hands aside and stepped free of them quickly.

Standing in front of her, his cock straight and hard, he was magnificent.

"Please," she begged. "Make love to me."

"As you wish." He leaned over her, claimed her

mouth in a long, hard kiss, then blazed a trail down her neck, across her collarbone and over the swell of her right breast to capture a nipple between his teeth.

Flicking and rolling it, he brought her close to the edge.

Sunny ran her fingers over his hair and clutched the back of his neck, urging him to take more.

Dash moved to the left breast and gave it the same core-tightening treatment.

Far from sleepy, Sunny was so tense, she felt she was perched at the edge of a precipice, ready to fly over it. But he wasn't quite done, yet.

Abandoning her breasts, Dash moved south, tasting every rib with his tongue. When he reached the juncture of her thighs, he parted her knees with his and dropped to a kneeling position on the floor.

Her breath coming in short, ragged gasps, Sunny waited for his next move, afraid it would send her flying over the edge too quickly. More afraid he would stop and leave her hanging. "Please," she whispered.

He chuckled, the warmth of his breath against her inner thighs sending shivers across her skin. With his thumbs, he parted her folds and tapped her clit with the tip of his finger.

"Yes," she said.

"You like that?" he asked.

"Oh, yes," she moaned.

"You'll like this better," he said and took that little

nubbin of flesh into his mouth, flicking it with his warm, damp tongue.

Sunny's back arched away from the mattress. It would only take one more flick...

He gave it to her and sent her catapulting over the edge. Wave after wave of sensations rocked her all the way to her core. The tingling started there and worked its way outward to the very tips of her fingers and toes.

Her body pulsed with her release. Sunny rode the wave all the way to the very end. When she fell back to earth, she drew in a deep, unsteady breath, and then another, before she could speak a single word.

"Wow," was all she could push past her vocal cords.

"That's all you can say?" he said with a wink.

She nodded. "You took my breath away so completely."

Sunny gripped his shoulders and pulled him up her body. He scooted her up on the bed and settled between her legs, leaning on his arms as he hovered over her. He nibbled on her earlobe and whispered. "Had enough?"

"No. Not nearly," she said. "I want you. Now. Inside me."

"As you wish." Dash leaned back, applied a condom, and then eased into her channel so slowly it was excruciating.

Sunny held her breath, adjusting to his incredible

thickness. Impatient to have him all the way inside, she gripped his tight ass and slammed him home.

He drove deep and held, allowing her the time to accommodate him.

Having him inside wasn't enough; Sunny wanted more. She wanted him to explode with the same intensity she'd experienced. She wanted to know she'd brought him to the brink and beyond.

With her hands still on his muscular buttocks, she guided him in and out, increasing the speed until he took control and thrust again and again.

Beneath her fingers, his body tensed, his muscles grew rigid. He drove into her one more time, hard and fast, burying himself deeply.

His cock throbbed against her channel as he remained above her, his jaw hard, his gaze pinning hers. When his orgasm waned, he dropped down to seal her lips with a kiss.

She opened to him, meeting his tongue with hers, tasting her sex on him. Heat coiled again at her core, but she wasn't ready to go at it again. As much as she'd loved it, she knew she needed to sleep. There would more time to make love with this incredible man. At least, until she left Afghanistan.

As scary as the country was, Sunny wasn't ready to leave. Not if it meant leaving Dash behind. How could two people with such different careers make a relationship work?

Assuming he wanted this to continue past Afghanistan.

For all Sunny knew, Dash was only in it for a quick fling. He'd been upfront with her. He wouldn't have a long-term relationship, wouldn't marry or have children, until he could be home to see and help them grow.

"Why are you sad?" he asked, kissing her eye lids.

"Who said I was sad?"

"You have a little frown between your eyebrows. Not enough to be mad, but enough to be sad. Was it not as good for you as it was for me?"

"Oh, sweet heaven," she exclaimed. "It was great."

"But?"

"I'm not ready to go back to the States," she blurted out.

"Who said you were going back? You still have two more stops before your tour is over."

"I know." Sunny stared at his chin, instead of his eyes which seemed to see everything. "I'm just getting to know you. I don't want this to end."

He pressed his forehead to hers. "I feel the same."

"Seriously?" she asked, looking up into his eyes. "You feel the same?"

He nodded. "I know I have only two more stops with you, and then you're on your way back. I don't know when I'll be back stateside, but when I do go, I'll be at Fort Hood, Texas. You'll be wherever they schedule your next concert."

Sadness filled her at the thought. "What if I want to see you again? I don't even know where you live."

"I live in Killeen, Texas, close to Fort Hood, when I'm not deployed," he said. "What if I want to see you again? Where *do* you live?"

She laughed. "I live in Austin, where I grew up with my grandparents." Her heart already felt lighter, knowing he was only a few miles down the road from her home.

"That's practically next door." He gathered her close and rolled them both onto their sides, his staff slipping free of her.

They lay for a long time, touching each other.

"You should go to sleep," he said.

"I want to stay awake. I'm afraid if I wake up, I'll realize this was all a dream, and you'll be gone." She twirled her finger over the hard brown button of his nipple.

"Sweetheart, I'm not a dream. Some would consider me a nightmare," he said with a grin. "I'll be here when you wake."

She yawned, exhaustion claiming her. "Promise?"

"I promise," he whispered and kissed her forehead.

Sunny slipped into the darkness of sleep, Dash's arms wrapped around her. Her last thought as she drifted away was that she could love going to sleep like this every night.

CHAPTER 10

For the next thirty minutes, Dash held Sunny in his arms, watching her chest rise and fall, her hair splayed across the pillow.

He'd only known this woman a short time, but that instant connection couldn't be denied. All the years he'd pushed off long-term relationships, he'd rationalized it by saying it was the job that kept him from committing. In reality, he hadn't found the right woman. The one who made his heart sing and his blood burn with desire.

Now, after only a little more than twenty-four hours, he had the woman of his dreams in his arms, and he wanted the entire package—her, a home, children and a life together.

The more he thought about it, the more he realized it was impossible. But when had he ever given up on the impossible? They'd said it would be too hard for him to make it into Delta Force. He'd met that impossible challenge and had excelled as an operative.

His relationship with Sunny was entirely different. They were from such different worlds, it would be more than a challenge to make the two worlds come together. One of them would have to give up their career or a major portion of their career to make a life together happen.

Dash could get out of Delta Force or take a training position and remain in one location until he retired at twenty years. Hell, being on the team wasn't something one did forever. But was he ready to give it up? He loved the men he worked with. They were his brothers.

He couldn't ask Sunny to give up a stellar career as a recording artist. She'd worked hard to get where she was and deserved to shine in the spotlight for as long as her fans kept buying her recordings.

His thoughts churning, he couldn't sleep. Eventually, he rose from the bed, dressed in his uniform trousers, T-shirt and boots. It wasn't like he'd go back to sleep. Not with so much on his mind.

Once he'd dressed, he paced the length of the motorhome, wondering if the guys on the night shift were having difficulty staying awake while Dash was having trouble sleeping. He was about to go out and check on them when a knock sounded on the door.

He pushed aside the curtain and looked down at

his buddy, Rucker. Relieved to see a familiar face, he opened the door and stepped out into the night.

"I didn't expect you to answer the door so fast," Rucker said. "I was afraid I'd wake you from sleeping."

"I was awake. What's up?" Dash asked.

"Got word from the CO. Through their interviews with the women and children who'd been captured for resell, the intelligence community has learned a little more about the man who is orchestrating these deals."

"Yeah? Who is he?"

Rucker drew in a deep breath and let it out. "They don't actually have a name, just a description."

"That's better than nothing. As long as he doesn't have the same description as Joe Smith Afghan with dark hair and dark eyes."

"You're in luck. Most of the women said he was tall and had light blue or gray eyes. They couldn't see his hair because he always wore a hat pulled down over it. He spoke English with an American accent."

"So all we have now is that he's got gray or blue eyes."

"Yeah. I know it's not much to go on. The other thing is we got a cleanup team out to the sight where your convoy was attacked. They found one of the motorcycles they used. It was allegedly stolen from a job site run by a US-based contractor."

"Did they track down the contractor?"

"By phone. He said, those motorcycles had been stolen over a month ago, along with a delivery truck. The truck was the one in which they were transporting that group of women and children."

"It probably is the same group responsible for the attack and the kidnapped women."

"That's what the Intel guys are saying. I agree."

Dash frowned. "I just wonder how they got away with six motorcycles and a truck, without getting caught."

"Yeah. Sounds suspicious to me."

"Isn't there a network of contractors here in Afghanistan?" Dash asked.

"I would assume so. They probably know who's out here and call on each other when they need help."

"Did you talk to the contractor, Desmond Housman, here at this FOB? Maybe he knows something about the thefts."

Rucker nodded. "We looked for him, but he was only on the base for the day. As soon as the concert was over, he bugged out." Dash's team lead grinned. "He probably only came to watch Miss Daye sing."

"Can't blame him." Dash said. "The woman has talent."

"Yes, she does." Rucker tipped his head toward the motorhome door. "How's she holding up?"

"As well as can be expected for someone who has gone through what she's experienced and given a two-hour concert." As well as making love like a wildcat.

Dash didn't add that, but the laundry list of what Sunny had endured was enough to make a weaker woman cry.

"I've had the team out safeguarding the perimeter during the concert. They're still out there looking for trouble. I hope they don't find it. You might want to wear your radio communications device through the rest of the night. I've got a hinky feeling."

"Hinky?" Dash grinned. "Since when do you say hinky?"

"I picked it up from Nora," Rucker said. "Fine. I have a gut feeling that all is not well. I've been all over this base and can't put my finger on one single thing."

"I don't know about you being hinky," Dash's grin broadened, "but your gut is rarely wrong."

"Keep your eyes and ears open." He nodded to each end of the motorhome. "Your bodyguards are one man short. Paul is filling in for Marcus since he's out due to his injury. He'll pull an all-nighter with Stewy and Ron, switching out in an hour. I'll have our guys come provide backup at that time in case Paul gets too sleepy to be effective."

"Thanks," Dash said. "I feel better with our own team providing security."

"I can get them here in a few minutes."

"I'd like that."

"Consider it done." Rucker turned. "Keep safe. I'll be back in an hour to check on things."

After Rucker left, Dash waved at Paul at one end of the coach and turned to wave at Stewy. Then he went back inside to make a cup of coffee. It was going to be a long night.

He had a mug of water in the microwave when another knock sounded on the door.

Figuring it was Rucker, he gave a quick glance through the window anyway.

Instead of Rucker, Floyd stood there, a nervous look on his face.

Dash opened the door. "Mr. Pendleton, what brings you here this late."

"I was just out checking the line. Where are your bodyguards?" Floyd asked. He darted a look to the right as if he was worried someone would come at him.

Dash stepped down one step and glanced to the right. Stewy wasn't in the same position he'd been just moments before.

When he looked the other direction, he heard a sound from inside the motorhome.

He turned to check it out when something hit him in the back.

Fiery pain rippled through him and rendered his muscles useless. He collapsed into the coach, his head hitting the side of a cabinet. Pain shot through his temple as he lay immobile on the floor. He couldn't move, couldn't do anything.

Someone lifted his legs and tried to drag him out of the motorhome.

"We don't have time," someone said. "Just close the door and go!"

The slam of the driver's and passenger's door echoed through the coach, and the engine roared to life.

A man stepped over him, dragged his legs into the coach and shut the door. He kicked him in the side, sending a burst of pain through Dash.

"You'll re...gret..." he forced out.

"I doubt it. Not when the price for your pretty singer is over a million dollars."

The voice sounded familiar, but Dash couldn't quite put his finger on who it was. Not someone he knew personally, but someone he'd recently met.

Lying face-down, Dash couldn't see who was talking. He couldn't turn his head to identify the men.

Though his body had shut down, Dash's mind kept churning. The tall man with the gray eyes the women had described could be Desmond Housman. The work he was doing for the military as a contractor gave him access to a lot of different bases in Afghanistan.

The bastard.

He willed his arms and legs to work, but they were useless.

"What did you do with the tour dude?" said a man

with an east coast accent. The two men were near the front of the motor home.

"He saw my face," the man Dash figured was Housman said. "Yeah. He had to go."

"What about the two bodyguards?" the east coast dude said.

"They didn't see me. I hit one with the taser. Jones gave the other one the same. They might be shaking out of it soon. All the more reason to get the hell off this base as quickly as possible," Housman said. "Did you secure the gold mine?"

East Coast Dude chuckled. "The girl? Not yet. I'll do that now."

The motor coach lurched and started moving.

"We're going through the fence," Housman said. "Hold on and be ready to get down if the sentries start shooting. But since we're leaving, they might not be as inclined to fire on us, especially since we're in a motorhome."

East Coast Dude stepped over Dash and into his view. "What should we do about this guy?"

"When we ditch this bus, we'll burn it, with him in it."

Damn. If he was going to get out of this situation alive, the taser's effect needed to wear off quickly. And he would get out of this alive. The woman he was falling in love with was about to be kidnapped and sold to someone willing to pay a million dollars for her.

No wonder Housman was so determined to catch her.

A little tingling started in his fingers and toes. He still couldn't move them, but it gave him hope. If they just didn't make the transfer until he had use of his body, he'd find a way out of this mess. How the hell had he let them get to him? He was better than that.

Until he'd lost focus, making love to a beautiful woman.

CHAPTER 11

SUNNY WOKE to the sound of the engine rumbling beneath her. She stretched and felt the empty space beside her. The door to the bedroom was closed. Dash must have gotten up when the crew left the base.

She dressed quickly in jeans and a white blouse, buttoning it as she fished for her shoes in the closet.

Once she was dressed, she glanced at the digital clock on the nightstand. Three o'clock in the morning?

She could hear voices on the other side of the door and was curious to find out why they were leaving so early.

As she reached for the doorhandle, she heard an unfamiliar voice say, "Did you secure the gold mine?"

Another equally unfamiliar voice responded, "The girl? Not yet. I'll do that now."

Secure the girl?

The only girl she knew was the only one in the motorhome.

Her.

What did they mean by "gold mine?"

Then it came to her. She was the gold mine. The girl they were to secure.

Where was Dash? Had they killed him to get to her?

Her heart raced as she searched the room for something with which to defend herself. All she had in the bedroom was a blanket, pillows, clothes and shoes. Nothing that could stop a full grown man from knocking her around and tying her up.

Then her gaze skimmed across her guitar on the stand in the corner. It wasn't heavy enough to knock a man out, but it could stun him long enough to let her get by.

She grabbed the guitar by the neck as the door to the bedroom opened.

Because she was standing behind the door, the man coming through didn't see her as she swung the guitar, crashing it over his head.

He went down, cursing.

Sunny leaped over his hunched body.

At the same time, the motorhome sped up as if racing across the base. Through the living room seating area, she could see out the front windshield. They were approaching the perimeter gate.

Two MPs stood in front of them waving their hands.

Instead of slowing, the driver punched the accelerator, making the lumbering coach go even faster.

The MPs dove to each side to avoid being run over.

The coach broke through the gate and the barriers, rocking the big beast of a vehicle right then left.

Sunny fell to the floor where she found Dash's inert form.

Her heart squeezed hard in her chest as she scrambled to find a pulse. When she did, she almost cried.

He was alive. But why wasn't he moving?

A man near the front turned toward her, a frown setting between his eyebrows. "What the hell?"

He raised his hand and pointed a weapon at Sunny's chest.

Sunny dove as he pulled the trigger.

"Fuck!" a voice called out behind her.

She turned to see the taser wires clinging to the chest of the man she'd hit with the guitar.

Good. He'd be out of commission for a few minutes at least, giving her time to figure out what to do about the man wielding the taser.

The motorhome burst out into the open, racing through the darkness. They wouldn't get far in the big vehicle. Others could easily catch up to them, once they learned the coach had been hijacked.

Sunny just had to stay alert and keep the man with the taser distracted until help caught up with them.

A foot bounced against her ankle. She jerked back but realized quickly it was Dash. He must have been tased and was just starting to come out of the temporary paralysis.

"Pocket," he gritted out.

She dropped to her knees beside Dash. "What did you say?"

"Pocket," he whispered.

She scrambled to find whatever he wanted her to fetch when her fingers closed around a small handgun. She pulled it free and tucked it into the front of her jeans, covering it with her blouse before she straightened.

The tall man with the gray hair and gray eyes, and holding the empty taser gun, sneered at her. "All I got to say is my buyer better pay up. You've been nothing but a pain in my ass from the git go."

Sunny recognized the face and the voice from their meeting earlier. "Desmond Housman."

He nodded his head and pulled a gun from a holster beneath his jacket.

"You can't shoot me," Sunny said. "I'm your golden ticket."

"You're right. But I can shoot your lover. He's worth nothing to me."

Sunny stepped between Housman and Dash. "You'll have to shoot me first."

"No," Dash said from the floor, his body rocking side to side, if only slightly.

"Shh, Hayes," Sunny said. "Housman and I are having a discussion."

"That's right. Your woman is spunky as well as talented. The sheik footing the bill will have his hands full with this one in his harem."

"He won't have his hands full of me," Sunny said. "I'm not going anywhere with you or anyone else selling human beings like cattle. You're a despicable man."

"I might be despicable," Housman said. "But this sale will allow me to retire to a little island in the south Pacific. I won't have to beat the bushes in Afghanistan ever again."

"You didn't have to in the first place," Sunny said. "Selling human beings is the lowest of lows a man can sink." All she had to do was keep him talking until the Deltas arrived to save them. She'd only resort to shooting Dash's gun if the situation got worse.

Out of the corner of her eye, she could see Dash's legs twitch. He rocked from side to side, gaining momentum. His arms were still useless, but his legs were just beginning to move

Sunny couldn't count on Dash's help in his

current condition. She'd just have to figure her way out of this mess and save her Delta at the same time.

"Boss, there's headlights behind us," the driver called out.

"Ignore them and keep going. We meet up with our transfer six kilometers from the base. They're heavily armed."

"Boss," the driver said, "they're almost on us."

"They won't do anything to jeopardize Miss Daye." Housman leveled his gun on Sunny. "Keep moving. There's one million dollars waiting for us if we get her there alive."

Headlights flashed in the window to Sunny's left as a vehicle passed. Machine gun fire erupted, loud and insistent.

The motor coach swerved, throwing Sunny and Housman across the room. She landed on her hands and knees, the gun in her waistband popping out and skittering across the floor, out of her reach.

Damn. Her only method of protecting herself and Dash was too far for her to dive for. Or could she?

"Don't even think about it." Housman was on his feet again, holding onto the cabinet beside his head with one hand and his gun in the other. "If you make a move toward that gun, I'll shoot your lover."

Sunny grabbed the seat next to her and pulled herself to a standing position, placing her body in front of Dash's.

Another burst of machine gun fire sounded on the other side of the coach.

Again, the motorhome swerved.

Sunny held onto the chair, refusing to go down again.

Housman was equally successful remaining upright.

The motorhome slowed, making a horrible sound like metal on concrete.

"Why are you slowing?" Housman yelled.

"Both front tires have been destroyed. This bus won't go any farther."

"Make it go. We can limp along on the bare wheels if we have to."

"Not in a crate this size."

"No," Housman shouted, "we can't give up now." His face creased in an evil sneer. "It's my money. I'll deliver her one way or another."

As the coach came to a squealing halt on the road, Housman lurched toward Sunny.

She backed away a few steps, until her foot bumped the gun she'd dropped.

"I wouldn't reach for that. As soon as you do, I'll put a bullet through Hayes's head," Housman warned.

"All this for money?" Sunny asked. "Is it worth it?"

"When I'm sitting on a beach in Tahiti, sipping Mai Tai's, it'll be worth it. Until then, you're a damned pain in my ass." He reached for her.

She jerked backward.

His hand grabbed a hunk of her hair, and he yanked her toward him.

As he did, she kicked the gun backward, toward Dash's hand and prayed.

Now would be a good time for him to recover use of his arms, especially his shooting arm.

CHAPTER 12

THE WHOLE TIME Sunny argued with Housman, Dash was working the numbness out of his arms and legs. He still didn't have full use of them, but he might have enough.

When the motorhome swerved, he was able to turn his head in the direction of Housman. When the contractor grabbed Sunny's hair, and she kicked the handgun toward Dash, he managed to close his fingers around the grip. With every ounce of strength and concentration, he focused on lifting his arm enough to aim the weapon.

The problem was that Sunny was now in the line of fire. He couldn't shoot without taking the chance of hitting her. With his body still semi-immobile, he couldn't just shift his position. He had to wait for an opportunity. In the meantime, he couldn't let Housman see that he'd snagged the gun.

He slid the weapon beneath his leg and waited for Housman's next move.

It wasn't long before he made it. He pulled Sunny's head backward and snarled in her ear, "Not only are you my retirement account, you're my ticket out of here."

"I'm not going with you," she said.

"If you want Hayes to live, you will." He pointed his gun at Dash, pushing Sunny through the motorhome toward him and the door he lay in front of.

All Dash had to do was wait for Houseman to push Sunny past him, and he'd have him in his sights.

"Hey," the driver said, "I'm coming with you."

"You'll have to get behind me. Miss Daye is my shield. They won't shoot with her this close."

Dash didn't correct the man. He lay still as if the paralysis was still in effect. He didn't even dare to say a word in case Housman decided to shoot him after all. If he died, Housman might just get away with Sunny.

That would not happen. Not on Dash's watch. He'd already fallen victim to the bastard; he'd take him down if it was with the last breath he took.

Housman shoved Sunny forward. She stumbled on Dash's leg and would have fallen, except for the contractor's hand in her hair holding her up.

As she passed by him, Dash moved his hand from beneath his leg. Housman was so busy watching

Sunny open the door, he didn't see the gun come out and aim upward.

But the man behind him saw it and yelled, "Watch out!"

Dash pulled the trigger.

Housman jerked backward. The bullet tore through the arm holding Sunny by the hair. Immediately, his grip slackened, and Sunny pushed open the door and fell through.

Housman roared and turned his gun toward Dash. But Dash had more use of his arm by then. He'd raised it high enough to hit the man in the chest this time. The bullet ripped through the man's heart, and he dropped where he stood, his eyes wide as if he were surprised his plans had been foiled.

The driver whipped his hands in the air. "Don't shoot. I surrender."

Rucker leaped up into the coach, his rifle aimed at the driver.

Dash let his arm fall to the floor, relief washing over him. "You're a sight for sore eyes, Rucker."

"Shoot, Dash, we leave you to guard the talent, and I find you lying down on the job." He kept his weapon trained on the driver.

"Had a rough night," Dash said. "Give me a few minutes, and I'll be right as rain. You might want to get the other guy out of here before the taser wears off him."

Rucker laughed. "Always wondered what it would feel like to be tased."

"You should try it sometime. We could use the one Housman used on me," Dash suggested.

Sunny poked her head back in the door. "Dash?"

Dash lifted his head. "I'm okay."

"I heard gunfire," Sunny said.

"I got Housman," Dash said.

"Good. That bastard deserved to die for what he was doing," she said, her expression fierce. "Are you going to be able to get up?"

"In time," he said.

"Want some company until then?"

He smiled. "You know I do. We have a lot to discuss about the road between Austin and Killeen."

She nodded, a smile spreading across her face. "Yes, we do."

THE DELTAS HELPED CARRY Dash to one of the vehicles for transport back to the base. Sunny sat beside him and helped him balance until he got back full control of his muscles.

By the time they reached the base, Dash was well on the way to a full recovery, and the sun was rising in the east.

So, his knees buckled a little when he stood, but he was able to walk to the mess tent where Dash, the Deltas and the USO team were treated to breakfast while they waited for the motor pool to tow the big motorhome back to the base. They determined the tires and wheels were shot, and they couldn't get replacements anytime soon, so they would have to tow it to the next location.

Dash and Sunny were offered a ride in the tow truck or one of the other vehicles in the USO caravan, but they opted for the comfort of the towed motorhome.

"You want us to ride with you?" Rucker asked.

"No way. It would be easier for you to protect us riding on the outside," Dash said, trying to suppress a smile.

"Yeah," Rucker said with a knowing nod. "You just want to be alone with Miss Daye."

"Damn right, I do," he said, slipping his arm around her.

"We have a lot to discuss," Sunny said, smiling up into Dash's eyes. "I'm thinking of moving north."

"North?" Rucker asked.

"North of Austin, where I currently live," she said. "I think Killeen will be far enough and still keep me in Texas." She winked.

"I see how it is," Rucker grinned. "Nora will be happy to have another female to hang out with at our Sunday barbeques."

Sunny raised an eyebrow. "Nora?"

"Nora's Rucker's woman," Dash said. "She's an Army nurse."

"I look forward to meeting her," Sunny said.

"And you will. As soon as we get back to the great state of Texas." Dash held the door to the motorhome open and helped Sunny up into it since it was jacked up at an odd angle. Once she was inside, he climbed up into the living area and pulled her into his arms.

Sunny wrapped her arms around his neck and leaned up to brush her lips across his. "We've only just met, but I feel like I've known you for years."

"We've lived a few lifetimes in the past couple days. Kind of like cats." He brushed a strand of her hair back behind her ear. "Think we could be falling in love?"

She laughed and squeezed him tight. "I'd say it's a definite possibility."

"Good, because I'm about to break all my self-imposed rules, and I think love is as good an excuse as any."

"It's the best one I can think of," she said breathlessly.

"I think I love you, Sunny Daye."

"I know I love you, Ryan Hayes."

"I think that needs a kiss to seal that deal."

"You're right."

He crushed her to him and kissed her like there might be no tomorrow.

The way their luck had been running, that was a possibility. Why waste any more time when they could love in the moment?

THE END

Interested in more military romance stories?
Subscribe to my newsletter and receive the Military
Heroes Box Set
Subscribe Here

SEAL JUSTICE

BROTHERHOOD PROTECTORS BOOK #13

New York Times & *USA Today*
Bestselling Author

ELLE JAMES

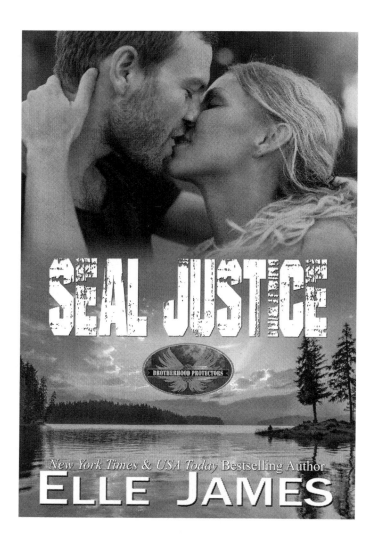

SEAL JUSTICE

BROTHERHOOD PROTECTORS

New York Times & USA Today Bestselling Author

ELLE JAMES

CHAPTER 1

REGGIE MCDONALD HELD her breath and listened for him. She shivered, her naked body chilled by the cool damp air of her prison. Though her brain was murky, her thoughts unclear, and her strength diminished, she knew what she had to do. When she could hear no sounds of boots on the wooden steps leading down into the earthen cellar, she continued digging. Inch by inch, she scraped away at the soil of her cell, praying she was correct in assuming hers was on the edge of the group of cells. If she dug long enough, she might see daylight and find a way to escape the hell she'd been trapped in for what felt like a lifetime.

Using the tin cup she'd been given to drink from, she scooped dirt from the corner behind the door. That small space was hidden from her captor when he came to feed her or shackle her to take her up to the big house where he tortured her and the other young women he'd kidnapped and held in the horrible dungeon beneath his house.

If she got out, she'd find help to get the other women out and save them from the sociopath who forced them to bow to his bidding. If they didn't do what he said, he whipped them with a riding crop or shocked them with a cattle prod. Sometimes, he burned them with the lit end of the cigars he smoked.

To keep them pliant to his will, he drugged their food and water, making them weak and groggy, unable to form clear thoughts or fight back.

Reggie had caught on to what he'd been doing. She couldn't quit eating or drinking completely, but she'd skip a day and use that time of semi-clear thinking to work through the problem to come up with a solution. On those clear days, she'd acted just as drugged when she'd been shackled and taken up the wooden stairs to the Master's house. When she could see out a window, she'd determined the house sat on the side of a hill, the slope dipping downward from the back of the structure. Though the women were trapped in the cellar, the earthen walls of their prison couldn't be that thick, especially on the far end where she was being kept. The hill sloped sharply on that end, giving her hope that, with steady digging, she'd eventually break free of captivity and escape.

Reggie prayed she was correct and scooped faster, pushing the soil she'd dislodged into the sides of the walls and floor, packing it down so that her captor couldn't tell it was fresh dirt.

She paused again as a sound penetrated the wooden door of her cell.

Footsteps.

"He's coming," a voice whispered. Reggie recognized Terri's voice. She was in the first cell, closest to the stairs. She'd been there the longest. A single mother of a little girl, she'd held out all those days, suffering through the torture in hope of seeing her little girl again. Lately, she'd fallen into despair of ever escaping.

Quiet sobs sounded from other cells along the row.

Reggie emptied her cup, quickly patted the dirt she'd removed into the ground, dragged her tattered blanket over her naked body and moved to the opposite corner where she curled up and pretended to be asleep.

Boots clunked down the steps to the bottom.

Silence reigned, even the few sobs ceased as the women held their breath, praying the Master wouldn't choose them for the trip up the stairs.

Reggie waited, listening. When a door hinge creaked, she braced herself.

"Please, no. Please," a woman's voice pleaded with the Master. It was Beth, a young college student who'd been captured on her way home from a night class. "Don't hurt me," she cried.

"Shut up and move," the Master's harsh voice echoed in the darkness.

"No, please. I can't." The sharp crackle of electricity sparking was followed by a scream.

Reggie winced and bit down hard on her tongue to keep from yelling at the man for hurting Beth. She couldn't draw attention to herself. Not now. Not when the hole she'd been digging was already two feet wide and as deep. If he took Beth up to the house, he'd be distracted long enough Reggie might finally break through.

Beth cried as she stumbled up the stairs, the Master's footsteps sounding as he climbed up behind her.

As soon as the door clicked closed at the top of the stairs, Reggie grabbed her cup and went back to work, digging furiously, scraping the dirt away with the cup and her fingernails. The Master usually kept a woman up in the big house for at least an hour before he brought her back to her cell. She didn't have much time.

She abandoned quiet for speed and dug as fast as she could.

"What are you doing?" Terri whispered, her voice barely carrying above the scraping sound of the cup on dirt and rocks.

Reggie ignored her, determined to get as far as she could before the Master returned.

Her cup struck a large rock. Undeterred, she

scraped around the edges, her heart beating faster, her breath coming in ragged gasps. The drugs in her body slowed her down, making her want to crawl into her blanket and sleep. But she couldn't.

"Stop whatever you're doing," Terri said.

Reggie halted and listened. When she didn't hear footsteps or the quiet sobs of Beth being returned to her cell, she went back to work on digging around the rock.

Soon, she found the edge of one end of the stone and worked her way around it.

After scraping and digging for what felt like an hour, she poked through the dirt and felt cool, fresh air streaming through a tiny hole onto her fingertips.

Not trusting her hands, she pushed her head through the tunnel and sniffed fresh air, the scent of decaying foliage a welcome scent from the earthen cell. She inhaled deeply, her breath catching on a sob. She'd been right. Her cell was on the edge of the hill. If she dug a little more, she might be able to push through. The large rock was in the way. If only...

She pulled her head out of the tunnel and shoved her bare feet in and pushed as hard as she could.

The rock didn't move.

Lying on her back, the cool dirt floor making her shiver, she scooted closer, bunched her legs and kicked hard with her heels, over and over until the rock moved. Hope blossomed in her chest and gave her the strength to keep pushing and kicking.

"You have to stop," Terri said. "When one of us crosses him, he punishes us all."

Another one of the women sobbed. "Please don't make him mad."

Reggie didn't want any of them to be hurt by her actions, but the Master was hurting them every time he took one of them up into the house. She had to get out and get help for all of them. Using every last bit of her strength to kick and shove at the boulder until it rocked and gave, she finally pushed it free of the soil, and it rolled down the hill. Loose dirt fell into the tunnel, blocking the sweet scent of fresh air.

Using her feet again, Reggie pushed at the dirt. More fell into the gap. She scrambled around and shoved her arms through the tight tunnel and patted the loose dirt against the walls of the tunnel, shoving the excess out and down the hill.

"Shh!" Someone said from one of the other cells. "He's coming."

A door opened above them. Sobs sounded as Beth descended into her prison, followed by the clumping sound of the Master's boots.

Reggie hadn't taken the time to pat the dirt into the walls this time. If the Master came into her cell, he'd catch her at digging her way out. She looked through the hole. Gray beckoned her. She shoved her shoulders through the tunnel. It was tight. Really tight. But if she could get her shoulders through, she could get the rest of her body through. Desperately inching and wiggling her way inside, she prayed she could breach the exit before the Master jerked open her door, grabbed her by the ankles and yanked her back inside. He'd beat her and chain her. And he'd throw her into the wooden box beneath the stairs where he kept the "naughty" girls.

No way. She couldn't let that happen. Not when she could taste freedom.

With her body blocking the tunnel, sounds of weeping and cries were muffled. Reggie couldn't tell if the women were informing the Master of her scratching and digging. She wasn't sticking around to find out. Once her shoulders were free, she braced her hands on the edges of the hole and pushed as hard as she could. Her body scraped through until her hips were free of the tunnel. Grabbing onto nearby branches, she pulled her legs out of the hole. Once all of her was free, gravity took hold, and she tumbled down the hill, her skin torn and gouged by sticks, rocks and bramble.

The jabs and tears made her cry out with joy. The pain wasn't inflicted by the Master but delivered by nature as a testament she was out of that hell.

She came to a stop when her head hit the big rock she'd pushed free of her tunnel. For a long moment, she lay still, her vision blurring, pain raking through the base of her skull.

Then she heard the sounds of dogs barking, and her heart froze. The Master had two vicious looking

Rottweilers he'd kept tethered when he'd brought her up into the big house.

Reggie staggered to her bare feet and shivered. The cool night air wrapped around her naked body. Swallowing the sobs rising up her throat, she ran, following the hill downward. She didn't know where she was or which way to go, only that she had to get as far away from the house and the dogs as possible. She hadn't come this far to be ripped apart by his maniacal dogs or dragged back to house and beaten until she couldn't remember who she was or why she cared.

Sticks and rocks dug into the soft pads of her feet, drawing blood. She kept running until her feet were as numb as her skin and mind. The dogs were getting closer. She had to do something to lose them.

The hill continued downward. A cloud crossed over the sky, blocking what little starlight penetrated the tree branches. Her lungs burning and her heart beating so fast she thought it might explode out of her chest, Reggie was forced to stop long enough for the cloud to shift, allowing the starlight to illuminate her way.

When it did, she stared out at a dark canyon. She stood on the edge of a precipice. Easing to the edge, she could see the glint of starlight off what appeared to be a river forty feet below where she stood.

The barking dogs were close now.

Reggie turned right then left. No matter which

way she went, the cliffs were still as high as the one in front of her. She couldn't backtrack. The dogs were so close enough, they'd find her.

She refused to give up. But what else could she do? Die from the vicious rendering of sharp Rottweiler teeth, go back willingly to the Master's house to be beaten, or jump off a cliff into water of which she had no idea of the depth?

When the barking sounded right behind her, Reggie spun to face the two Rottweilers, emerging from the tree line...stalking her.

A shout from behind them made her heart leap into her throat. The Master.

Without further thought or mental debate, Reggie turned and threw herself over the cliff.

As she plunged downward, she steeled herself for the impact against rocks or whatever lay beneath the water's surface.

Crossing her arms over her chest, pointed her toes and hit the river feet-first, sinking deep. The chill shocked her body, but she kept her mouth shut tight, and struggled, kicking hard to rise. Just when she thought she would never breathe again, she bobbed to the surface and gasped. Above her, she heard the wild barking of the Rottweilers.

The cold water helped clear her foggy brain. She had to make the Master think she was dead. Taking a deep breath, she lay over, face-first in the water and floated as far as she could before turning her head to the side to take another breath. She did this for as long as she could hear the dogs barking above. The Master had to think she'd died in the fall from the cliff. It was the only way to get away and make him think she couldn't tell the authorities about what he had hidden in his basement.

After a while, the sound of the dogs barking faded. Knowing the dogs couldn't follow her scent in the water, she let the river's current carry her along as she treaded water to keep her head above the surface.

The cold sapped what little energy she had left. She rolled onto her back and floated into the shallows where she dragged herself up onto the shore.

Darkness surrounded her, embraced her and sucked her under. As she faded into unconsciousness, her last thought was...*I'm free*.

ABOUT THE AUTHOR

ELLE JAMES also writing as MYLA JACKSON is a *New York Times* and *USA Today* Bestselling author of books including cowboys, intrigues and paranormal adventures that keep her readers on the edges of their seats. When she's not at her computer, she's traveling, snow skiing, boating, or riding her ATV, dreaming up new stories. Learn more about Elle James at www.ellejames.com

Website | Facebook | Twitter | GoodReads | Newsletter | BookBub | Amazon

Or visit her alter ego Myla Jackson at mylajackson.com
Website | Facebook | Twitter | Newsletter

Follow Me!
www.ellejames.com
ellejames@ellejames.com

Bride Protector SEAL (#2)

Montana D-Force (#3)

Cowboy D-Force (#4)

Montana Ranger (#5)

Montana Dog Soldier (#6)

Montana SEAL Daddy (#7)

Montana Ranger's Wedding Vow (#8)

Montana SEAL Undercover Daddy (#9)

Cape Cod SEAL Rescue (#10)

Montana SEAL Friendly Fire (#11)

Montana SEAL's Mail-Order Bride (#12)

SEAL Justice (#13)

Ranger Creed (#14)

Delta Force Rescue (#15)

Montana Rescue (Sleeper SEAL)

Hot SEAL Salty Dog (SEALs in Paradise)

Hot SEAL Bachelor Party (SEALs in Paradise)

Brotherhood Protectors Vol 1

The Outrider Series
Homicide at Whiskey Gulch (#1)

Hellfire Series
Hellfire, Texas (#1)

Justice Burning (#2)

Smoldering Desire (#3)

Hellfire in High Heels (#4)

Playing With Fire (#5)

Up in Flames (#6)

Total Meltdown (#7)

Take No Prisoners Series

SEAL's Honor (#1)

SEAL'S Desire (#2)

SEAL's Embrace (#3)

SEAL's Obsession (#4)

SEAL's Proposal (#5)

SEAL's Seduction (#6)

SEAL'S Defiance (#7)

SEAL's Deception (#8)

SEAL's Deliverance (#9)

SEAL's Ultimate Challenge (#10)

Billionaire Online Dating Service

The Billionaire Husband Test (#1)

The Billionaire Cinderella Test (#2)

The Billionaire Bride Test (#3)

The Billionaire Daddy Test (#4)

The Billionaire Matchmaker Test (#5)

The Billionaire Glitch Date (#6)

The Billionaire Perfect Date (#7) coming soon

The Billionaire Replacement Date (#8) coming soon

The Billionaire Wedding Date (#9) coming soon

Hearts & Heroes Series

Wyatt's War (#1)

Mack's Witness (#2)

Ronin's Return (#3)

Sam's Surrender (#4)

Cajun Magic Mystery Series

Voodoo on the Bayou (#1)

Voodoo for Two (#2)

Deja Voodoo (#3)

Cajun Magic Mysteries Books 1-3

Texas Billionaire Club

Tarzan & Janine (#1)

Something To Talk About (#2)

Who's Your Daddy (#3)

Love & War (#4)

Declan's Defenders

Marine Force Recon (#1)

Show of Force (#2)

Full Force (#3)

Driving Force (#4)

Tactical Force (#5)

Disruptive Force (#6)

Mission: Six

One Intrepid SEAL

Two Dauntless Hearts

Three Courageous Words

Four Relentless Days

Five Ways to Surrender

Six Minutes to Midnight

Ballistic Cowboy

Hot Combat (#1)

Hot Target (#2)

Hot Zone (#3)

Hot Velocity (#4)

SEAL Of My Own

Navy SEAL Survival

Navy SEAL Captive

Navy SEAL To Die For

Navy SEAL Six Pack

Devil's Shroud Series

Deadly Reckoning (#1)

Boys Behaving Badly Anthology

Rogues (#1)

Blue Collar (#2)

Pirates (#3)

Stranded (#4)

First Responder (#5)

Blown Away

Warrior's Conquest

Enslaved by the Viking Short Story

Conquests

Smokin' Hot Firemen

Protecting the Colton Bride

Protecting the Colton Bride & Colton's Cowboy Code

Heir to Murder

Secret Service Rescue

High Octane Heroes

Haunted

Engaged with the Boss

Cowboy Brigade

Time Raiders: The Whisper

Bundle of Trouble

Killer Body

Operation XOXO

An Unexpected Clue

Baby Bling

Under Suspicion, With Child

Texas-Size Secrets

Cowboy Sanctuary

Lakota Baby

Dakota Meltdown

Beneath the Texas Moon

Made in the USA
Middletown, DE
27 February 2023

25816956R00115